Islands of
Decolonial
Love

Stories & Songs

Islands of Decolonial Love

by Leanne Betasamosake Simpson

ARP BOOKS • WINNIPEG

Copyright ©2015 Leanne Betasamosake Simpson

ARP BOOKS (Arbeiter Ring Publishing)
201e-121 Osborne Street
Winnipeg, Manitoba
Canada R3L 1Y4
arpbooks.org

Printed in Canada by Imprimerie Gauvin
Cover image "Letter to William" by Bonnie Devine
Courtesy of Gallery Connexion, Fredericton, NB
Typeset by Urbanink
Tenth printing, February 2022

 MANITOBA ARTS COUNCIL
CONSEIL DES ARTS DU MANITOBA

 Conseil des Arts Canada Council
du Canada   for the Arts

 Canadian   Patrimoine   Manitoba
Heritage   canadien

ARP acknowledges the financial support of our publishing activities by Manitoba
Culture, Heritage, and Tourism, and the Government of Canada through the
Canada Book Fund.

ARP acknowledges the support of the Province of Manitoba through the Book
Publishing Tax Credit and the Book Publisher Marketing Assistance Program.

We acknowledge the support of the Canada Council for our publishing program.

With the generous support of the Manitoba Arts Council.

Printed on paper from 50% recycled post-consumer waste.

Library and Archives Canada Cataloguing in Publication

Betasamosake Simpson, Leanne, 1971-, author

Islands of decolonial love / Leanne Betasamosake Simpson.

ISBN 978-1-894037-88-4 (pbk.)

I. Title.

PS8637.I4865I75 2013   C813'.6   C2013-906100-2

still, i am not tragic

—lee maracle, "blind justice"

i have to tell you something, i said.
i'm not going to lie.
i have to tell you.
i have this god-shaped hole in my
heart, and i think you do too.

—richard van camp, *the lesser blessed*

the kind of love that i was interested in, that my characters long for intuitively, is the only kind of love that could liberate them from that horrible legacy of colonial violence. i am speaking about decolonial love… is it possible to love one's broken-by-the-coloniality-of-power self in another broken-by-the-coloniality-of-power person?

—junot díaz, *boston globe*

Contents

📼   All pieces featuring this logo are also musical collaborations, which can be streamed and downloaded at **arpbooks.org/islands**

indinawemaaganidog/
all of my relatives

i am standing on the wharf in cap saint louis just wondering, when a guy i've never met shows up. you should know i make it a policy not to talk to people unless absolutely necessary which is judgmental and damaged and yes i miss out on possibility, but at the same time tricky people do manage on occasion to penetrate my aural perimeter. it all works out in the end. sort of.

so etienne shows up and says allo and obviously he knows i'm not suppose to be there so i'm suspicious of what he wants. i tell him i want to see the seal colony even though that's not what i want and that's not what i'm looking for. he immediately says he'll take me. i ask how much. he says for free.

fine.

nothing in life is free. the best things in life are free. there is no such thing as a free lunch.

we walk down the dock and he offers his hand so i can step down onto the deck of the boat. of course i refuse and step down onto stacked broken plastic bins on my own because we need to get a few things straight right from the beginning and this is one of them.

he starts the engine and i'm in the back with the gear so we can't talk. it's sunny and it's windy and it's perfect and as we drive away from the shore i think about dexter and all the possible scenarios. he interrupts, offering me a coors light iced tea and i take one on impulse even though its only ten thirty in the morning and coors light is always gross. suddenly we're a mile off shore in the atlantic.

we drive past a kayaker and kumbaya plays in my head and i stand up and wave like a happy person so he'll remember me when the cops question him later.

it's only a few more minutes to the seals which are herded on a sand bar so they can catch the fish moving into the river with big tides. we get close and they stampede into the sea reminding me of dogs and sheep and buffalo and etienne asks me if i want to go farther.

with the same impulse as the coors light iced tea, i say yes and he says he knows this place where there is a school of mackerel. we could fish because last night he was there and he caught a thousand pounds just jigging for them. i decide he is mi'kmaq because he could be and even though that probably means nothing it makes me feel less nervous.

on the way to the mackerel, etienne tells me how the feds kicked his family out of the park and paid them three hundred and fifty bucks for their land in 1968 and then they bulldozed the house. i tell etienne that i know how that feels but i don't think he believes me because he thinks i'm from toronto and i'm rich and judgmental and full of shit because that's what people think when you say the word "ontario."

etienne gets out the lines and in two minutes we know we're on the school because we're pulling in mackerel easy. he watches as i hold the hook and snap the fish into the garbage pail, which is my reveal. it's sunny and it's windy and it's perfect and the arms of the day are wide open and no one has to be anywhere. i see a northern gannet and i love gannets because they can disconnect their wings before they plummet into the sea after a fish. imagine disconnecting a body part! the gannet swims over to the boat smelling the fish blood and etienne hands the gannet a fish and says "the bird is my family, all of this, the fish, the seals, the water—this is my family," which is his reveal.

our eyes meet because now he has my attention. i walk over and hug him and he is the kind of person that can give and receive a real hug and i'm not one of those people because my alarm system goes off when people touch me and i freeze up and shut down. this time that doesn't happen. i decide to kiss him and it's perfect and easy and we make out void of awkwardness but with a clearly defined beginning and a clearly defined ending. then he drives back to shore while i gut the fish in the back of the boat using his terrifyingly sharp knife, feeding the guts to the gulls and the gannets. he drops me off on the dock. we thank each other. we say goodbye and i pay attention to each step, instead of looking back.

she hid him in
her bones

i am lying down flat on my back on the ice of chemung. the wind is water falling over my frame, borrowing the parts i can't hang onto.

he tells me he wants to die really slowly so he doesn't miss anything. i tell him i'm not that brave, i want to miss everything.

the ice-wind is singing a single, suspended note with no phrasing, no breath and a benevolent intensity.

he talks about disconnecting slowly—a methodic retreat into the background. in a different breath, he talks about fighting like hell to the end of everything.

the hole in the ice is healing into slush and the line is starting to freeze. i make the inside wind and the outside breath the same temperature.

he's reading the signs and forecasting tomorrow. i'm taking inventory of unasked questions, wondering which holds the most regret.

he starts the truck and tells me to get in. i say, "i'll walk." he nods, shuts the door and then drives off the ice, stopping to wait until i turn towards the shore.

binesiwag

*y*ou are eight years old and your mom decides it's time you stay overnight at her relatives, for no particular reason other than it is a milestone she needs to stroke off on her child development checklist, and you fucking hate the idea and there is enough anxiety in your stomach to power the electricity needs of southern ontario well into the next generation, but your mom says you are going anyway and you decide to pray to god to intervene because it is the only thing you can think of that can save you and because for some reason you don't understand, santa claus and the tooth fairy are not real but god is, apparently.

your mom loads you and your sister into her dark green dodge station wagon with fake wood paneling on the sides and she drives you first to ingersoll and then to kitchener for the sleepover, which at this point is juvenile detention in your mind and this is confirmed by the weather because it's august and the humidity is smothering you in the backseat, your bare legs stuck to the vinyl seating, the windows all down, even the one at the very back.

you pray all the way to ingersoll because god likes persistence and you are not a quitter, and even though your prayer repertoire is weak and uninspired you know that inspiration doesn't move the god you have been introduced to, persistence and hard work and sacrifice do, so you stop thinking about it and resume the lord's prayer interspersed with "dear god, please, please don't let her leave me at auntie marvelous' for the weekend."

you are on the 401 when the sky begins to get much too dark for four in the afternoon and your mom says in an adventurous suck it up way, "we're heading into the eye of the storm," right before you see a magnificent flock of hawk-sized shingle birds taking off, their hold defeated and severed from the flat roof of a warehouse.

it starts to rain with the violence of any mid-summer thunderstorm, there is lightning, not the sheet or heat lightning you are used to, but fork lightning, the wind is everywhere and so your mom pulls the car over because the visibility is too poor to drive, her hands gripping the steering wheel like the strength in her fingers are the only thing keeping the car upright.

your mom turns around from the driver's seat and yells, "roll up in a ball if the car tips over," which at this point hadn't occurred to any of you in the back seat, but your mom soldiers on trying to pull her knees around the steering wheel and towards her chest to demonstrate.

the sound is the loudest sound you've ever heard, like the amplified sound of an old vacuum before anyone knew you could lose your hearing through prolonged loud sound exposure, and it is so loud you can and do scream as loud as you want and no one can hear you.

you scream "i don't want to go to auntie's," over and over.

you don't scream "please save us" or "i don't want to die yet."

the worst of it is over within minutes, and your mom pulls the car back onto the 401, gawkily driving past wire fencing, crumpled transports lying on their sides and through overpasses reduced to rubble—the corn stalks are standing bare and alone in the fields, their leaves harvested.

you are thinking that surely there is no way you are going to auntie marvelous' after that weather apocalypse and you wait with raw anxiety for the cancellation, but your mom doesn't say anything about what just happened or about changing plans.

she just drives on to auntie's, drops you and your sister off and leaves, with you standing on the suburban burnt lawn, the dead blades of grass pricking your toes, you wondering for the first time if god really does exist, or if perhaps it is possible that your mom wields more power than him.

later that night, the news tells your mom that the you were one hundred metres from death in the f4 tornado that touched down on the 401.

your mom tells you you're fine, you're fine, you're fine the next time it thunders but your sister thinks she's full of shit and goes berserk and when no adults can calm her down they get you, and for the rest of your life you wish that you'd known to hold her and to whisper into her ear that binesiwag are always only here to protect us. they are only ever here to love us.

nishnaabemowin: binesiwag means thunderbirds.

leaks

dirt road
open windows

beautiful one, too perfect for this world

the immediacy of mosquitoes
humidity choking breath

my beautiful singing bird

five year old ogichidaakwe
crying silent, petrified tears in the backseat
until the dam finally bursts

*you are the breath over the ice on the lake. you are the one
the grandmothers sing to through the rapids. you are the
saved seeds of allies. you are the space between embraces*

she's always going to remember this

you are rebellion, resistance, re-imagination

her body will remember

*you are dug up roads, 27-day standoffs, the foil of industry
prospectors*

she can't speak about it for a year, which is 1/6 of her life

*for every one of your questions there is a story hidden in the
skin of the forest. use them as flint, fodder, love songs, medicine. you are from a place of unflinching power, the holder
of our stories, the one who speaks up*

the chance for spoken up words drowned in ambush

you are not a vessel for white settler shame,

even if i am the housing that failed you.

---

nishnaabemowin: ogichidaakwe is holy woman.

21

waaseyaaban

*W*hen we got to vegas we camped in the stardust hotel's parking lot. a white guy from kentucky in the rv next to us helped my mom pull out the ends of our tent trailer, while i cranked the thing up. for a week my mom cooked our meals on the coleman stove with stuff she took out of the blue cooler. we got up early, because the nevada sun beating down on the black tarmac made the tent trailer a lot hotter than it had ever been in the bush. during the day, we swam in the indoor pool at the stardust hotel, and we walked around looking for groceries and camp fuel, neither of which were easy to find.

the parking lot of the stardust hotel had a building with toilets, sinks and a pay shower for the campers to use, and on the sixth day, my mom paid twenty-five cents in american money for the four of us to have one shower, in which she instructed us to wash ourselves and our five pairs of dirty underwear. we hung our underwear on yellow rope that my mom attached to one end of the trailer and then tied to a hydro pole at the other. i got out the digital watch i'd found in the bathroom and sat on the tarmac, timing how fast the hot thirsty air dried my underwear.

on the morning of the seventh day, the same man from kentucky helped my mom push the sides of the trailer back in, i cranked it down and we left, heading north and east. utah and colorado went by fast and just over the nebraska border, i started to see signs for carhenge. my ten-year-old mind decided to direct the car to carhenge, the mythical stone spiritual site made by ancient druids. it was the kind of spiritual intervention we all needed, that i thought everyone needed really. by six o'clock my mom was looking for a place to camp anyway so i carefully mapped her to the town of alliance and the sunset rv park, a homage to burnt grass, dying saplings and thin plastic lawn ornaments in amongst streets of decomposing white vinyl trailers.

it turned out carhenge was an exact replica of stonehenge, so i felt less of a let down when the campground lady told me stonehenge was in england. exact replica wasn't quite true though, because carhenge was made out of old cars, spray-painted grey. mom said it was ridiculous. my brothers were completely disinterested. so after they all fell asleep, i climbed out of the wing of the trailer and i headed to carhenge, with my toy birch bark canoe clutched in my sweaty kid hand.

i slept with canoe every night because without it there was only insomnia. i didn't drag it around like some kids dragged around blankets, but i did look very forward to seeing it each night. it was always in my corner, and i liked that.

really, it was more than that. i loved it more than i loved anything else or anyone else. i did. i do. without canoe i felt like i was suffocating and unraveling and it was unbearable. but with it, i was effortless in a lake of calm.

when i got to carhenge that airy nebraskan night, i traced my finger along the plaque indicating that jim reinders had built the sculpture as a memorial to his dad. i tried to imagine the moments that had piled up against each other to result in this: the thirty-eight old cars to build the circle, the three standing trilithons within the circle, the heel stone, slaughter stone, two station stones and the aubrey circle. i walked into the middle of the circle, the cars holding up sky like scaffolding. i laid down in the middle in a fetal position. me and my canoe.

it was the sheriff that found me, waking me up by placing his hand on my right shoulder and mumbling "fucking redskins."

i kicked him in the shins, banking on the protection of a ten-year-old's body and a shred of honour on his part.

i yelled "fucking cops," because it felt good.

i noticed the first light before dawn, waaseyaaban sneaking around to back light his gun, because we are anything but stupid.

in the weight of it all—my mom defending me to the sheriff, the sheriff threatening to book me for assault, the relentless sun—i'd left, forgetting canoe on the dead prairie, alone in the middle of the spectacular nothing.

we drove straight home staying in crappy roadside motels instead of rv parks.

it was going to be months before i could get canoe back. i couldn't breathe at the thought.

letters. searches. mail.
distance. time. memory.

canoe finally came home, swaddled in plastic bubble wrap and in a small cardboard coffin with american stamps and the word fragile written on the outside of the box. reunnion was one of relief mostly. the smell of ok, the cocoon of someone who's always got your back. i decided to never take canoe outside again. mom agreed, and then she asked if it would be ok to take it out, just one more time, to celebrate its return.

mom, canoe and i sat in the front seat as she drove us through the fall, along a dirt road lined with blood-red maples past the entrance to the dump. it was late in the season, the leaves would drop any day now. we watched from the car as groups of four or five white tundra swans, wings un-crumpled, danced in the air over the piles of rotting garbage, and then returned to their comrades resting on the fall-brown field, on their way south. on their way to something better.

---

nishnaabemowin: waaseyaaban means the light at dawn, the first light, before dawn.

giiwedinong

i t wasn't until the next day that people arrived and began chipping the frozen blood that had dripped out of his ears and onto the ice. the ice was melted in a curved depression where his body had lain while mrs. thornhill, a nurse and the lead for the other team performed unsuccessful cpr on him until the volunteer fire department arrived twenty minutes later. i don't know why they didn't move him off the ice, but they didn't, and so the ice's memory preserved for us the precise minute his aneurism burst, a fraction of a second after his right foot lost contact with the hack. looking at the ice depression, i decided that was a perfect time to die. collecting the momentum, the release, the glide, and then floating delicately towards the stopping place.

giiwedinong and i had joined our high school curling team two weeks before because mr. tanner said we needed life skills. we didn't know what that meant, but we didn't let that stop us. giiwedinong perched on tip toes and ran a hand over the top of the ledge of the back door at the club just after the first practice. the key was found and by the end of the first session we'd learned how to turn on the lights. so that night after giiwedinong's dad died, we used the key to enter the rink after everyone else had gone home. we lay down on our backs on the pea-green indoor/outdoor carpeting that surrounded the third sheet of ice. we looked up, because we didn't know what else to do.

after a couple of hours, we loaded the one red stone giiwedinong's dad had in his hand when he died into the back of giiwedinong's pickup truck and we drove it onto the rez. for the next week, we threw that thing on the lake practicing the deliveries mr. tanner had taught us. one time the rock almost went through old man za's ice fishing hole. another time it hit a goose hard enough that we had to go home for the gun. we never talked. we just stayed out on the lake throwing that thing over and over.

mr. tanner was our coach. he was also the math teacher and the shop teacher and he wore cheap suits from tiptop tailor, short sleeved white dress shirts and jackets with patches on the elbows. sometimes at the end of summer he told us, "you can get a whole suit, tie and everything for $29.99. you can't beat it." we believed him. but we also hoped never to be in the position of having to acquire our own town clothes. mr. tanner kept trying to make giiwedinong the skip because he thought giiwedinong might be smart, but giiwedinong didn't take an interest. giiwedinong didn't like the pressure. we weren't there to think.

the funeral was the same as every other funeral we'd been to that year. they stuck to hymns and read bible verses nobody understood to gently bore us into a grieving coma. when it was all over we drank church punch and ate egg salad sandwiches the ladies' auxiliary had made in the church basement.

on monday at school, giiwedinong wasn't in homeroom but making an announcement over the intercom thanking everyone for their support. i didn't recognize giiwedinong's voice as it came hollowly into the classroom carrying nervous, masked raw emotion to our ears. tuesday we were off school for the county high school curling championship and so we'd be at the curling club all day. giiwedinong would be able to ease back into things on wednesday. mr. tanner stopped me in the hall on my way to the locker to assure me that giiwedinong and i wouldn't have to play on sheet three and that some of the guys were going out tonight to make sure all the blood was gone.

the next day, mr. tanner announced on the way out of school that he was wearing his lucky brown corduroy curling pants, which he seemed to forget were in his regular rotation and we saw them at least three times a week. we were familiar with the worn-out right knee. he'd booked a van to drive us to curling club, and after we'd arrived at school on the bus, we waited in the smoking section for him to pick us up. the day passed. i was freezing. the kids from the other schools had real plastic sliders. we had duct tape, but we still managed to make fun of them because they could afford equipment and because they were from big cities and they knew fuck all about the rez or us.

eventually it was the last game of the day. there were four sheets of ice in the town's curling club that spanned the length of the building. the other divisions were holding their finals on sheets one, two and four. that left sheet three for us, complete with the shadowed but repaired impression of giiwedinong's dad. i could tell because mr. tanner was bounding towards me and giiwedinong with force. he passed us and said "follow me." we did. we went through the brown and orange shag carpeted change room, with windows looking out onto the ice surface, up the stairs and across the laminate dance floor to the bar. then we went behind the bar, and he got out three glasses. giiwedinong and i stared at the floor but we heard him with tongs and ice. then he got the bottle of rye out and poured us triples. "here," was all he said. we raised the glasses up on his cue and drank the rye, letting it burn down past our knees, and then we followed him back down the stairs and onto sheet three.

giiwedinong threw take-out weight straight down the centre of the house regardless of where the yellow rocks were. expressionless, every rock giiwedinong threw went right through the house, for the entire game, even when we had the hammer.

after that game we never went back to the curling club to lie on the ice again. we had to go back for wedding receptions and retirement parties and events like that because it was the only available space except for church basements, and you weren't supposed to drink in those. but neither of us set foot on the ice for the rest of high school.

a few years got lost. giiwedinong and i were separated. we eventually met up again at college in the city because i needed a place to live and giiwedinong had an extra room. so we were roommates for a while and then, of course, we weren't just roommates.

after it happened, giiwedinong apologized a hundred times. we played the scenario over and over like cops combing the evidence for the piece we were missing. we were walking home from downtown, side by side, on wellington street, a busy four-lane road. i was explaining something using hand gestures, we can't remember what, when i mistakenly nicked the corner of giiwedinong's eye. a fraction of a second later, i was collapsing off the curb, my shoulder feeling like it had exploded, dented with the impression of giiwedinong's fist, landing on my back in a lane of traffic. giiwedinong rushed towards me to help and apologize and help. i got up and then we walked home, through a long tunnel of suburban nothingness. the walk was quiet, but the world was noisy. i tried to drown in quiet, but waves of "you have to's" and "it will happen again" and "no second chances" were relentless. i knew that getting hit like that was suppose to be traumatic, so i acted like it was even though i actually didn't feel anything at all.

***

the next time i saw giiwedinong was back at home during the town's fall fair. i ran into giiwedinong's mom, nona, first.

"hey you, it's been a long time," she said hugging me.

nona was over six feet tall, with thick silver hair, cut into a short pixie cut. she was wearing navy blue knee highs up to her knees, with a red massey ferguson shell. we were in front of a metallic roller coaster for kids. the tractor pull was about to start and the announcer was rounding up the crowd. her greenest eyes were sparkling in the noon day light. i wondered what she remembered about me. i remembered her boiled eggs and how she got so mad at giiwedinong's dad one time that she chopped the apple tree he'd given her for their anniversary down with four swings of the axe in front of a crowd of kids. then i saw giiwedinong. there was a toddler in a backpack, and an earthy partner and the grandma. giiwedinong looked funny—dressed like someone who worked for the ministry of natural resources.

"hey you, it's been a long time," giiwedinong said hugging me.

i pushed my closed lips to giiwedinong during the hug, because if anything, i believe in being clear.

---

nishnaabemowin: giiwedinong means in the north; it also refers to a place that is home.

smallpox, anyone

i. the blanket

she wrapped a woman up
in a blanket from the bay
and rolled her down a hill
to remind everyone
that blankets are for swaddling
and not for smallpox.

i went down the very same hill
with wet mittens and soggy boots
on a plastic toboggan,
a foodland bag,
a cardboard box
and my raincoat.

> *the teacher is telling me i should feel proud because toboggan
> is an indian word. i am telling the teacher that out of every-
> thing, this is a strange thing to feel proud about, but she's
> disagrees: "i think your cultural heritage is a mighty fine thing
> to feel proud about leanne and i think it will lead to great
> success in your studies."*

ii. rising to the occasion

the duke and duchess were coming to visit
and all she had to wear
were ripped jeans and black t-shirts
so she made a dress with saucers for nipples and
a beaver lodge for a bustle.

> *if you would just read more post colonial theory, you'd un-
> derstand that your anger is part of the binary of colonialism
> and therefore colonial and if you just take some of the things*

from settlers and some of the things from your ancestors, you'll
find you can weave them into a really nice tapestry, which
will make the colonizers feel ambivalent and then you've
altered the power structure.

i liked the saucers for nipples idea so much that i start
wearing dinner plates around the house
over t-shirts

i liked the idea of wearing dinner plates
over t-shirts
so much that i start wearing dinner plates
over t-shirts and
under plaid shirts

mom starts shouting
into the phone
"she's wearing those dinner plates again"
starting off low and slow,
accelerating into a crescendo
of "plates again!"

iii. fountain

after the dress,
she made a fountain
but not the kind you throw money into
and wish to fall in love or win the lottery

the kind that says
hey, anishinaabekwewag are stuck in this
endless goddamn loop
and nobody gives a shit.

your work is polemic. if you could re-write the tone of this
article to avoid shaming canadians into a paralysis of guilt
and inaction we could move forward with the publication of
your article.

iv. fringe

it's montreal
and i think it's spring
because i remember
garbage on the sidewalk.

you start the sentence with
"the reclining figure in white people art ..."
and everyone stops listening.

he's mad because
he dropped his bagel
on the ground
and no other kids
have to go to
fucking art galleries.

she thinks the woman
in the light box looks cold
and starts talking about
growing up and
making hamster houses
out of old computers
for her job.

i'm wondering:
when i cut my back like that
can you sew me up
the same way with
the fringe and the beads?

v. gitchidaakwe's sign said:

I AM WORTH MORE
THAN 1 MILLION
DOLLARS
TO MY PEOPLE

---

nishnaabemowin: gitchidaakwe means holy woman.

this beautiful disaster

*y*ou moved in and paid the rent for ten years or something. moved in shit all over everywhere. piles of paper. the fiction section of the new yorker from 2003-2009. books stacked on the floor in towers: peace power and righteousness, the fourth world, the lesser blessed, tobacco wars. a guitar. a piano. a pair of brooks running shoes with a schedule. the bellows of an organ and three tops of piano keys. an ipod with 1546 songs on it and one song on repeat. a yeti mic. more books: conquest, what does justice look like, bobbie lee: indian rebel, tracks. a strong craving for carbohydrates. passing thoughts of vegetarianism. guilt. fish oil capsules. the instructions for how to get american netflix. a google calendar with bi-weekly visits to the psychologist. st. john's wort. homeopathics. bach flower remedies. the tea the medicine woman gave you when she predicted you wouldn't take her advice. coffee. the aeropress. the large bialetti that got melted to the burner. the small bialetti. the regular coffee maker. the plastic bodum.

the glass french press. the bonfire percolator. the aeropress' reusable filters. the paper filters. the useless stir stick. 10 km. regret. three packages of grey card coloured moleskin diaries. a nine-dollar pen from chapters. mukluks. green drink powder. all five seasons of six feet under. half a set list from the lowest of the low in 1998. 15 km. more books leaned up against the wall: distillery songs, jesus' son, stripmalling (with notes in the margins), persuasion nation, the elements of fucking style. the grade 8 conservatory of toronto piano repertoire from 1968. a half-eaten bowl of cereal with co-agulating soya milk. an armband for the ipod. unopened mail. a drum. a shaker. a pipe. the claw of an eagle. anxiety. a down sleeping bag. the tent. a swiss army knife. 22 km. more books: this is how (this is not how), calming your anxious mind, this is how you lose her (it is), the idiots guide to emotional intelligence, lyrics and poems. five ojibwe-english dictionaries, no six. acidophilus. a lululemon bag with a hole in it. a case of sparkling water. the phrase: serotonin uptake inhibitors.

then we wait. you and me. me and you. us. the two of us. the one of us. i am you. you've become me. a beautiful disaster. i lie in bed. you hover. i remember being able to cry. you cloud. i wonder how much longer. you go into another room. it starts raining and you are glad, we are glad, i am glad. no more pressure. sleep moves out. for good.

so here we are again. we're always here again. saying nothing. doing nothing. now you've moved into november and february and tuesday. more books arrive by courier: these burning streets, come on all you ghosts (come on all you ghosts), green music. the birds go south. the air dries up. there are rescue attempts that you want but as soon as search and rescue leaves trenton, you put out your fire, and burry the flares. the lease never expires. the rent is always paid.

a pile of cedar. cold. fourteen saplings. hemp string. a blue plastic tarp. semaa. the pipe. the drum. the shaker. the eagle's claw. the east. one day. two days. three days. four days.

the fourth day, before that medicine man comes back i get up early. i masturbate. i justify it because probably the rules weren't explicit and plus how will he know. i finally fall asleep. you're right there as always. we're lying on a dock with our feet dangling in the lake. it's night. the stars are exhaling and we're watching. i never know how to start these things. we've never been good at eye contact. i'm wondering if i should. this seems perfect just lying here, feet wet, looking at the stars. why can't i just leave it alone? be in the moment for fuck sakes. everything's a goddamn project. i'm wondering why you're not starting. i think about straddling you. i decide against it. it needs to be more ambiguous. i imagine a commentator giving a play by play of my moves. i tell you i want to swim and i take off my clothes. you watch. i slip down off the dock into the water, turn around and move to your feet. you sit up. trickster smiles. your hands on the back of my neck. our tongues. two piles of clothes on a dock past midnight.

when i get home you've moved out of the house. not completely out, but into the spare bedroom. your stuff is spilling out from under the door. papers. magazines. spilt water. tea leaves. the door is bending. i reinforce it with my body, a flimsy dam, holding back the door as it bows.

---

nishnaabemowin: semaa means tobacco.

treaties

*a*t this particular point in time, the last thing you need is to be one of the only native kids, instead of the only native kid.

you are supposed to be studying biology but you are a horrible scientist—it was a happenstance escapist decision that had snowballed out of hand because of a lack of intervention on your part. after six years of university study, the only thing you know for sure was that "flammable" and "inflammable" both mean the same thing.

you are twenty-two.

there are a couple of problems with being twenty-two but you don't know about them yet, because you can only find out about the problems sometime after you are no longer twenty-two. anyway, one of the problems with being twenty-two is you start to get afraid that maybe you're horrible at everything, mostly because you're not really good at anything yet, so you decide to stay the course with biology until a sign appears, even though being stoned drunk all the time doesn't register as a sign.

the other problem with being twenty-two at university is that everyone gets mad and becomes a marxist and a buddhist and you are no exception because someone leaves a copy of zen and the art of motorcycle maintenance in the outhouse and you steal it and all of a sudden counting the number of dead alcohol-saturated ephemeroptera under a microscope becomes working for the man and capitalist and reductionist and the myth of objectivity, which propels you headlong into the loving uncommitted arms of art students, hippy musicians and pot—they've always liked ndns more than scientists do anyway and even fascinating romantic love is better than no love at all, except it's not that easy to orgasm. ok it is, but still. there's something missing. but you don't know yet, because you don't know what until you're thirty or forty or sometimes you don't get to find out at all.

so you sleep with a bunch of the hippy-artist-potheads and some of it's good and some of it's bad and some of them give good head and it's all a nice distraction while you spend the days counting juvenile salmon on the bottom of a stream somewhere north of here.

then it's halloween and the white kids dress up as the proletariat, and the rheostatics come to town and they play steve's tavern and by the end of the night the floor is a mixture of draft and costume debris and dave bidini wades through it all anyway with his acoustic guitar, long after the last encore, belting out the wreck of the edmund fitzgerald as he walks amongst the now disheveled audience, unconcerned with the fact that he is in land owned by stan rogers.

you stand still when he sings "gitche gumee" because it's the only almost nishnaabemowin you've heard since you moved here and you want dave to notice and to rescue you, and to pack you up in the rheostatics van and drive you back to ontario, and set you back up beside a big lake.

but that doesn't happen.

by now one of the hippy-artist-potheads you've been sleeping with is calling himself boyfriend which involves: 1. going to the bar and drinking pitchers of oscillating drink specials in a pizza delight-like setting 2. fucking. 3. telling him the shitty songs he writes are deep.

the two of you only deviate from the formula one time, and it was the time you got up and drove down the trans-canada towards halifax for no reason.

an hour down the highway, well past amherst, the car loses power and you find yourselves on the side of the highway as the winds pick up and the cbc tells you a hurricane is coming. a local in a truck stops and then comes back with a tow truck so he can tow your car to his friend's garage, which he says is a "certified vw repair centre."

the garage is a large rectangular metal shed. along one side, two women, girlfriends you presume, are hanging out on old couches by a wood stove. one of them brings you tea while you wait. your chair rocks back and forth like a meter while the mechanic works in front of you.

and now the bad news.

"the car is very hard to fix" he says in a thick german accent, "it needs parts. the switch is broken that shuts the battery off when the car is no longer running. that is the part you need, but it will take three days to get it here from halifax."

he pauses allowing you to feel the full impact of the prospect of being stuck in the living room of his garage for three days during a hurricane.

then he comes back with, "there is another option."

he says he can rig something up that can get us home. great. perfect. home. whatever that is.

three weeks later boyfriend breaks up with you because "fucking an indian was too much work." you regret ever looking him in the eye and marxism and biology, and dylan (doesn't stick) and buddhism and pot all at the same time. you call the only mi'kmaq you know. he's there in two hours flat and without turning off his car, he loads you into it and hands you a black coffee in a styrofoam cup. you move into the driver's seat while he kicks the shit out of the white guy that decided to be called boyfriend and then you drive away as soon as he's back beside you.

you ask him if he was gentle.

he shakes his head laughing and says "nishnaabeg." and then, "of course. hippies are fragile and his mom is probably some famous criminal lawyer in halifax."

you drive north through the bush of the mi'kmaq and maliseet. by dawn you turn your backs to the rising sun and drive along the big river towards mohawk territory. you look to the right, past the long black feathers on the wing, pulsing through the air, dancing through the clouds, thousands of metres above the river.

a year passes. courage coalesces. you take the train back, arriving to look things in the eye and leaving with the car and a box of detritus from a past life. by the time you reach thunder bay some white kids from winnipeg offer to buy the car for $2000 cash they made selling fimo beads at dead concerts. the regular household light switch the mechanic installed in the dashboard of the car so you "could turn off the battery when parked" is fascinating to them. they ask you if it is for switching dimensions.

and you look them in the eye and answer "totally."

pipty

i.

mike harris built a big concrete building on top of kinomagewapkong because he wanted to protect those teaching rocks from the rain. at least that's what his people said, but that can't be true because mike harris hates ndns, so why would he want to protect our teaching rocks? see. i told you. doesn't make sense.

"i want those fucking indians out of the park."

while he was building his big concrete building to protect the tourists from the rain, he blocked the creek and now we can't hear our ancestors talking to us, and some people say the spirits got stuck inside the building and some people say the spirits got stuck outside the building and some people say the spirits can move in and out of the building because after all, they are spirits. once those zhaganosh found out about those teaching rocks there was no way to project them because every time those zhaganosh find something special they can't leave it alone. they just can't.

dudley george is the first aboriginal person to be killed in a land rights dispute in canada since the 19th century.

i guess that's right, if you don't count suicide, cop killings, cancer, diabetes, heart disease, violent deaths, deaths from poverty, deaths from coping and deaths from being a woman.

    abaab: a key, to open with something, unlock,
    release, loosen

i'm standing on the dirt road outside of the park gate with every-one else waiting for someone to bring the key from the rez. this old woman gets out of her truck and she goes into the back because she keeps all kinds of stuff in the back and she comes out in her rubber boots and she walks right up to the chain link with her bolt cutters and she cuts that chain in half and moves it out of the way. then she doesn't even say anything, she just walks back to her truck and puts the bolt cutters in the back and drives back to the rez.

    aabaabika'ige: s/he unlocks

the profs from the native studies department are just silent because although we enjoy writing papers about this kind of thing, and although we like to discuss this sort of thing at conferences in casinos, while we complain there is no fair trade dark roast coffee, we do not actually enjoy being in the middle of events when they unfold.

ii.

"is there still a lot of press down there?"
"no, there's no one down there. just a great big fat fuck indian."

the night after dudley george got shot you came and picked me up and we drove to the ocean.

"the camera's rolling, eh?"

"yeah."

you were angry. you knew i'd know why. you knew i'd let you be angry, and you knew that i'd know it wasn't really angry anyway. it was a cover for hurt and sad.

"we had this plan, you know. we thought if we could get five or six cases of labatt's 50, we could bait them."

"yeah."

i think we fucked, and maybe I should say make love, but maybe not because we didn't actually make love. it was sadder than that. we were sadder than that. but it wasn't bad and it wasn't wrong. it wasn't desperate. i think it was salvation.

"then we'd have this big net at a pit."

"creative thinking."
"works in the [u.s.] south with watermelon."

you cried in my arms. when you were done crying, you handed me a 50, and i told you about how the old guys on the reserve called it "pipty" because there are no f's in ojibwe.

iii.

    abaab: a key, to open with something, unlock, release, loosen

    aabaabika'ige: s/he unlocks

and we never get to

    aabawe wendamoowin: to forgive, to warm up to or to loosen one's mind, to loosen or unlock one's feelings

---

nishnaabemowin: kinomagewapkong means teaching rocks and is the original name of the site at the petroglyphs provincial park, zhaganosh is a white person.

birds in a cage

*f*rom the time she set foot in her auntie's house her man was always phoning. she let it ring and ring like she wasn't home. the phone sat beside her ash tray, overflowing with butts and ashes and the rings seemed to get louder the longer she left it. eventually she'd pick up that phone and slam it down hard without speaking. then a minute or so would pass and he'd start again.

i meet her in a bar in fort william. i am just sitting there with my beer like i always do, not talking to nobody. she just waltzes in there and sits down beside me and starts talking like we're best friends. after a bit i can see that she is smart and strong and i like that so i keep on talking to her. she's telling me she just got back on the rez from edmonton. she left her man there because he don't treat her good. i can see that too because the skin under one of her brown eyes is too dark for just tired.

i think vera's beautiful and i mostly just stare at her when she talks. her brown eyes are both piercing and full of warmth at the same time. she has freckles and dimples and long, shiny black hair. her skin is flawless, and her sarcasm cuts through all the bullshit, as she calls it.

me and vera talk and talk that first night and she's girlier than me but i don't mind. i'm wearing a black t-shirt and jeans and docs like always and she doesn't seem to care either. the bar we're in reminds me of my grandparents' basement. it smells like stale beer and the floor in the hallway has circular tile like someone had glued silver dollars to the floor. the ceiling is covered with fishing nets that have dried starfish pinned to them. there is that false feeling of safety, tentative, like the place is within seconds of exploding.

me and vera talk and talk that second night and that third night and then that fourth week. the bar plays an endless loop of metallica, bon jovi, guns n' roses, ac/dc and stairway to heaven. it's going good, me and vera. no drama. no mess. it's easy. it's normal.

the next day at work the chief calls me into her office and tells me her niece is back and needs a break and so she wants me to hire her to fill out the stack of health surveys on my desks. it's an easy enough job. she goes around the rez and gets people to agree to participate. then she asks them a bunch of health-related questions and she marks their answers down in the space provided.

i tell the chief i am suppose to advertise for the position and interview so there is like no nepotism involved. the chief laughs. "hire vera," she says.

i hire vera.

a week later vera and i are at the ski jump behind the rez, the one you can see from highway 61. it was for the canada games, but then the games ended and they abandoned it and now there is a perfectly good ski jump in the back yard of the rez. vera took lessons or something when she was a kid. she tells me there isn't much to it as she is doing up my bindings. just let the wind carry you. keep your tips up. bend your knees when you land.

i'll tell you this: at the point in which your skis leave the snow, your body realizes it's flying and you wonder if you will just continue to just float up, despite everything you know about gravity.

i'll tell you this: once you've had this feeling, how can you stop yourself from wanting to do it over and over again?

after, i ask vera how the surveys are going.

she says "fine."

then she doesn't show up at the bar for awhile. i try to phone her and the phone just rings and rings like she isn't home. i can see her truck in the driveway of her aunt's house with the alberta plates. she's still here. i try to phone her and the phone just rings and rings like she isn't home. i can see her truck in the driveway of her aunt's house with the alberta plates. she's still here.

i feel as if i'm stalking her.

i knock on the door of the chief's office and go in. give her time, she says. personal problems, she says. tell the afn they'll get their surveys. back off.

i wait. i go to work. i go to the bar. i go to the ski jump.
i wait. i go to work. i go to the bar. i go to the ski jump.

finally, the chief walks by my office and pokes her head through my door. "vera says you can come over and pick up the surveys before she leaves."

"it's too late now."

"maybe it is," the chief says, "but go anyway."

i knock on the door of the chief's brand new house. vera answers and lets me in. i stand on the mat, numb, looking at the thick white carpet in the living room, the kind that shoes will never be allowed on. she gets the boxes of unfinished surveys from the basement. i thank her, open the door and step out into my breath on that cold february afternoon.

two days later, i'm looking out my office window and i see vera come out of the house, get into her black f150 with alberta plates and drive across the bridge, heading west.

two months later, i get into my truck and drive across that same bridge for the last time. i imagine vera sitting beside me, her bare feet on the dash, her cigarette hanging periodically out of the window while she fast forwards a cassette tape to the song she wants me to hear. my spine shifts as her lips touch mine.

and there is me, driving like she has unlocked one more bird from a cage, like her song is meant just for me.

identity impaired

i am worrying over the pile of mail we never open because somewhere in there is the post office slip telling me i have a registered letter.

in the apartment on reid street, the previous tenant stenciled a rose onto the wall. we had to paint over it, because i couldn't give birth staring at a stenciled rose.

registered mail means you've done something wrong, i tell him, plus my middle name is on the envelope, i add as more evidence.

the rose wouldn't leave, even after ten coats of paint, a parade of skull and cross bones carrying advice that chipped away nothing.

he recites the list of people that know my middle name over an endless loop of "happy birthday," coming from a card his grandmother sent him, except he can't hear the song unless he focuses everything and holds the card flat to his ear.

*the rose that won't leave stares at me, reminding me of tattoos
and trails of inflictive wounds that can't ever be repaired.*

i leave with the slip and the car keys.

*i can't remember how he got rid of the rose, but he did. then
after the baby and before the move, he embedded a stainless
steel disk into the hardwood floor to mark the spot where love
took its first breath.*

i hand the slip to the woman at the post office and she finds
the letter. inside the rectangular brown envelope regulated
words file by. i read the plastic card with status indian printed
beside my name, and the word slut is released, corroding my
veins, erasing my lungs, settling in a repeated singing outside
my ear drum.

he can't hear that singing either. even if he holds me flat to his ear.

lost in a world where he was always the only one

i did not want to drive onto the rez in a brand new white volvo turbo 680 or whatever the fuck it was called.

"why don't we drive in my truck, i'll submit the travel claim, it'll be easier."

"just get in, it's going to be great, we'll stop for breakfast on the way, this car has heated leather seats."

enthusiasm, like romance made me suspicious.

"your car's going to get dirty. the roads are rough. let me drive."

he explained the benefits of the heated leather seats.

"are you sure? i don't mind driving."

he retorted with the safety manifesto of volvo, and then with a firm "get in."

i slunk low into my heated leather seat in the rich, white car, clutching my tobacco, feeling the full impact of my betrayal, and knowing that technically things could still go either way, they were definitely heading in the wrong direction. i wondered if ira was a good guy, if i was just being judgmental and overly critical. i wondered how i could tell.

we drove out of thunder bay. it seemed to take forever to get to the terry fox monument and then to the turnoff for sibley. i smirked as we glided past the white vinyl-sided motel with the green trim by the turnoff, remembering someone else's story of a drunken three-way that happened in one of the rooms. it happened the third week in july with two co-workers. they got up the next morning, had breakfast together across the highway and then worked the rest of the summer like it had never happened, like the only witnesses were black velvet oil paintings, the smell of stale cigarette smoke and cable from alberta.

ira kept talking, about university politics, about maps, about quitting smoking. as we turned north at nipigon, past red rock first nation on lake helen, he told me his wife was giving him weekly workshops on how things in the house worked, like the bills and the washing machine, in case anything ever happened to her. i looked out the window, watching the hardness of those rock faces and imagining that serpent breaking the surface of the lake like an orca breaches for the tourists in vancouver. he explained his theory that white people had a plastic arrow tacked onto a piece of cardboard that they flicked to see which group of people they were going to screw over next, an arrow like you would flick to see how many spaces to move in a board game. according to him, jews and indians were on the board, and we never got to touch the arrow.

"those that never get to touch the arrow have to stick together, because you never know when your turn is coming," he explained.

i cringed every time he said "indian."

we continued past stands of black spruce, jack pine, abandoned snowmobiles and rusted trikes in front yards. i rolled down the window wondering what was going to happen when we got there. i imagined ideas falling out of my head into the swath of rubble between the highway and the rock face. ira continued talking, about his kids, who were my age, his wife and her garden, and about why i needed to go to grad school. i didn't tell him i wasn't smart.

the reserve we were going to is butted up against the trans-canada with cnr tracks dissecting it as well. we turned off the highway onto a dirt road in the immaculate white volvo 640 turbo with heated leather seats, my eyes barely over the dashboard, counting the four houses from the corner to locate the unmarked treatment centre, which was a regular empty inac house. i made a quick exit out of the car, thinking that maybe people wouldn't necessarily match me to the car if i put some clean distance between it and myself. the elders had told us to meet them there, and when we arrived, they were already gathering in the living room in a circle.

an old woman wearing a blue skirt, a plaid shirt, rubber boots with wool socks and a kerchief tied around her chin let us in. she told us to sit down on two aqua-blue folding chairs placed in the circle, and we did. everyone else sat on couches and uneven easy boys of varying shades of beige, blue and green. the linoleum floor was giving up, but there were curtains and flattened cardboard boxes for doormats. they started. they smudged, they prayed, they sang. they introduced themselves, and asked us to introduce ourselves. we did. i offered them my tobacco, apologetically. i lied and told them my grandmother told me to offer it to them. the only time my grandmother touched tobacco was when she was mixing it with weed. i was sure both my grandmother and my family would step up and support my lie at least existentially. i figured it wasn't much to ask, and more importantly it would be difficult for them to screw it up.

old lady levi then asked ira to speak and tell them about the project.

he lit a cigarette and he told them three things. first, that the band council had asked us to help the elders document all the ways they related to the land in the past and in contemporary times. second, that throughout the project, the elders would be in charge. they would make all of the decisions because as far as he was concerned, they were the experts, and third that the final document could be whatever they wanted.

then he sat down.

old lady levi stood up, thanked us and asked us to leave. she opened the living room door, watched us as we passed through it, and then told us to wait outside until she reappeared.

we did. for probably two hours.

we heard a lot of talking. some praying. some singing. some more talking.

ira smoked. i drank watery maxwell house out of a styrofoam cup, and then bit teeth marks all around the top edge, wondering what was going to happen to me when i hit the end of the prozac prescription no one was monitoring.

then we heard old lady levi's footsteps. she paused on the other side of the door. i imagined her hand on the handle, hesitating and then opening it.

we stood up.

she looked through us and said, "come back next month, maybe a monday next time. monday is better." she went back into the room and shut the door.

ira lit another cigarette, did up his coat, and walked outside, remotely starting the car on the way. it was nearly four, and the sun was sinking below the stand of black spruce out my window. we retraced our morning's steps back to thunder bay. a month later, this time on a monday, we went back, and we kept going back for two years, sometimes moving the meeting twice a month.

i redrew the maps those old ones kept tucked away in their bones.

i took these notes:

> *how to pluck the feathers off a goose*
> *how to roast a duck on an open fire*
> *how to block the cnr lines*
> *how to live as if it mattered*

when my head couldn't hold any more stories, gilbert brought the school bus around after he'd dropped the kids in town. all twenty elders piled in with ira and i, as they drove us down logging roads to the community's trap line.

remember:

> *to feel joy, you first have to escape.*

there's an old nishnaabe story, from the beginning of time, where seven grandparents who live in the sky world take a young child from his parents and raise him in the ways that the earth's people have forgotten. they teach him stories, songs and ceremonies and eventually he is sent back to earth to share these ways with his people. i never really liked that story, because my heart gets broken when they take the boy away from his parents, and i only ever listen to the rest in a nervous holding pattern, lost in how lonely that boy must have felt, lost in a world where he was always the only one.

jiimaanag

*y*ou are in the front of the canoe, paddling like a bugger with your skinny chicken arms to keep up with the rhythm of this old guy. you're on a spectacular lake or at least it used to be from what the old guy says, and even today it is a prairie of blue in all directions broken up by islands of birds and shield rock.

after you can't see the shore anymore, puck starts to tell you why he had the limp in his right leg. the story is more factual than confessional and you notice the sparseness of his words. he's speaking in english and you wonder why. if he was speaking in your own language the story would have been a poem instead of a newsletter, but you decide he's being deliberate. you decide maybe not everything needs to be a poem, maybe not all the time, anyway.

you already know the story he is telling you because his sister told it to you on the way back from the trapline last winter. still, you're listening and your mind is wandering all around it, searching for more. like how did he end up shooting himself anyway? and why was elsie the only one around to help? and how at twelve did she make the six-hour paddle across the lake? and what were the circumstances? circumstances.

"strong woman, elsie."

"oowaah."

"they took me to the hospital in winnipeg, and that's where i got this here limp," he finishes.

you laugh.

the canoe falls into silence again, except for puck's stories about the algae and the way the fish used to be. elsie told you he used to skate faster than the wind out on the lake day after day. the nuns were always coming to get him. she told you the hockey scouts came up from minnesota driving their big shot car out onto the lake to see him play. she told you the deal had been made, everyone's heads full of dreams for the anishinaabe kid that had never seen an arena.

"but we didn't lose him. that old bugger stayed," elsie had said as if it were a victory. the bullet wound, in her mind, was his savior even though he never skated again.

between you and him are the seven ribs of his canoe. you picture that fall day on the big island, before the shots were fired. the island, breathing large stands of jack pine and black spruce. the lake protecting the trees by acting like a moat, making it too costly to haul timber across the lake and down to the mill at fort alex.

several more hours of quiet paddle pass, and you arrive on the island meeting the boats of eighteen-year-olds that are your responsibility. puck doesn't waste any time unloading the canoe, and then he gets back into the seat, and says "see you tomorrow. i'll be back in the morning." he paddles off, without looking back.

the students are busy putting up tents and trying to get cell phone signals from the island. you're standing there looking at the line where the sky meets the lake, watching his silhouette disappear, believing that this is one of the places on earth that you can actually see the land curving.

you walk up the beach to the clearing where the kids were camping.

"where's puck?" says boss kid.

"he'll be back tomorrow," says you.

"where'd he go?"

"i dunno."

"he just left us here? with you? you're not even from here. you're like a mohawk or something."

"i guess."

"this is just fucking great. he's suppose to be here. he's getting the honourarium. this whole thing is disorganized and crap," says boss kid.

you set up your tent a deliberate distance from the students. the cook cooks. the students sneak into the bush to smoke up and make out. you follow, pretending the smell of weed is skunk and the making out is a friendly embrace.

you build a fire in one of the old fire pits. a couple of kids come over and cut pieces of logs and start competing with each other to see who can throw the log the farthest. everyone joins in. you throw a log.

after a few hours and a lot of laughing, boss kid decides to grow the fire. she cuts more wood, and makes the fire bigger. and then more wood, and then more wood. and in the dry tinder boreal of august, the fire quickly goes from a small campfire, to a bonfire, to a towering inferno.

the flames are now six feet tall.

then seven.

then eight.

then fifteen.

then thirty.

finally boss kid stops and says "you're just going to sit there and let us build this thing so big that the jack pine catches on fire and the island burns down?"

"it's not my island," you say.

"you don't care about us," boss kid hears.

nobody puts any more wood on the fire, instead bodies quiet on their mother as the stars wake up, and the winds die. night unfolds around you, and as the fire calms, you move closer. the moon rises over the lake and higher into the sky, watching, caring, bathing you in her warm light, a whip-poor-will, somewhere on the island, the only speaker.

* * *

elsie dies a few years later. there's regular church service, a wake and the burial in the graveyard behind the church. puck is absent from all that. he makes a point of never setting foot in churches, even for funerals.

the night before she is buried, you and puck launch the canoe in the dark behind the school. the weak parts of puck's plan hang between you like a clothes line with too much weight on it. it would only take one person to open the casket lid and all hell would break loose. you replace the body with rocks, stuffing old blankets and sleeping bags around them so they don't rattle when the casket is moved, but still. you shiver as you head towards the island without the faintest of visual clues, at least for you. the wind and water offer little resistance to any of this. elsie's body is between you, wrapped in grey wool blankets with only her makizinan showing. she'll be home, facing west, in the scaffolding in the trees in six hours.

nishnaabemowin: jiimaanag are spiritual as opposed to utilitarian canoes, makizinan are moccasins.

jiibay or aandizooke

all along the north shore of pimaadashkodeyaang
(you might call it rice lake)
all along the north shore of pimaadashkodeyaang,
are those burial mounds.
gore landing, roach point, sugar island,
cameron's point, hastings, le vesconte.
big mounds. ancient mounds.
mounds
that cradle the bones
of the ones that came before us.

this summer
this summer some settlers
who live right on the top of that burial mound in hastings,
right on top
were excavating

renovating
back hoeing
new deck. new patio. new view.

"please pass the salsa."

this summer some settlers
who live right on the top of that burial mound in hastings,
right on top
were excavating
renovating
back hoeing
new deck. new patio. new view.
and they found a skull.

call 911
there's a skull
call 911

there's more
call 911
jiibay.

breathe.
we're supposed to be on the lake.
breathe
we're supposed to be
gently knocking
and
gently parching
and
gently dancing
and
gently winnowing.

breathe.
we are
not
supposed to be

standing
on
this desecrated mound
looking
not looking
looking
not looking
looking
not looking
looking
not looking

did i see that right?
my skull is in a cardboard box
in that basement?
my bones are under

an orange tarp from canadian tire,
cracked.
rattling plastic in the wind.

my grave is desecrated
my skull is in that white lady's basement
my bones are under that orange tarp from canadian tire
cracked
rattling plastic in the wind like a rake on the sidewalk.

my body is tired
from carrying
the weight
of this zhaganashi's house.

ah nokomis
this shouldn't have happened.
your relatives took such good care.
the mound so clearly marked.
ah nokomis
how did this happen?
what have you come to tell us?
why are you here?

aahhhhh my zhaganashi
welcome to kina gchi nishnaabe-ogaming
enjoy your visit.
but like my elder says
please don't stay too long.

---

*nishnaabemowin: jiibay is a ghost, a skeleton, aandizooke a messenger, a being from
a traditional story, nokomis is grandmother, zhaganashi is a white person, kina gchi
nishnaabeg-ogaming is a mississauga nishnaabeg name for our homeland.*

she told him 10 000
years of everything

*t*he house had a makeshift feeling she should have grown out of a long time ago, her scattered belongings on the floor like residue. she liked to feel like she could leave at any moment just by throwing a few things into a bag. the truth was it would take her as long as anyone else to pack up and move, but the makeshift feeling was a feeling of being one step closer to escaping—the walls, the house, the city, and she liked that.

esther's home, her real home, was among the black spruce. she missed the labrador tea that edged the mossy bogs, the night sky that danced. like many people from the bush, work had led her to the city, and like those same people from the bush, she wasn't motivated by money, only by responsibility.

the phone rang and she stumbled to find it, tripping over toys and clothes heaped on the floor. remembering simpler times when receivers were attached to walls, she answered.

"hello?"

"aaniin esther! niin clarence."

it was clarence, he was taking language classes at the band office and never missed an opportunity to practice his rudimentary anishinaabemowin.

"hi clarence."

"aaniish na my beautiful sister?"

"i'm fine clarence. what's up?"

clarence launched into his news report from home, rhyming off his fact-based stories like she wasn't on the other end of the phone, in his best radio announcer voice. she half listened while she got dressed.

"... and nosh and wilma have called it quits. wilma's mom's got the kids until she gets back on her feet again," his voiced trailed off, waiting for some sort of acknowledgement from esther. esther wasn't listening, but clarence was undeterred. she only ever listened for one thing, and since sightings would have made the lead story, she felt safe in assuming there had been none. another week with no detection.

"holaaa clarence, that's a lot of stuff for one week," she said.

"no kidding sis, i don't miss a thing."

"but i gotta go, i'm going out tonight. the sitter is already here."

"you? going out? holaaa, hot date or what?"

"just an old friend coming through town, no big deal."

"k then, i'll keep you posted."

"kbye."

esther gave the sitter her number, hugged the kids and walked out into the cool summer air wearing an army jacket, a black t-shirt and jeans. she rarely left those kids, protecting them like mama bears protect their cubs.

she walked down the front step feeling too exhausted to be leaving the house, much less meeting her friend, but she knew that staying in wouldn't answer her questions. plus, this was her only chance to see him. his band was only in town tonight, and then he'd be gone again for goodness knows how long. it was now, or potentially never.

he wasn't actually a friend, not yet, anyways. she'd never met him in person. she was supposed to interview him for the left-leaning arts and culture weekly she freelanced for when she needed the $200. she knew him only through his music. he knew her only through her writing. her suspicions had always been aroused with him. first, from his gentleness and second from his honesty. he framed everything in the good, so gentle with whatever changes he thought maybe she should make. his quiet stillness endured even when her piece was a mess, hours before the deadline. but she had to be sure.

she walked the three blocks to the bar where he was playing. there was no line up to get in, which was a relief because waiting in a line at this point in her life seemed like a failure. she told the bouncer she was on the list. he looked surprised, but found her name on it and let her in. she headed straight for the bar to get a pint in hopes that it would both warm her up and calm her down. he found her.

"hey … are you esther?" he said softly.

"oh hey, hi, nice to meet you in person," she said shaking his hand.

"yeah, yeah. nice to finally meet you in person."

"totally."

"maybe we can hang out a bit after the gig … i know i'll be late …"

"that sounds wonderful."

"ok. wait for me."

"i'll wait."

she got another beer from the bar, waited for the opening act to finish and for the stage to be reset. a half hour later, he appeared on stage, guitar in hand. from the opening song, he seemed to focus directly on her. she tried to remember the last time she'd even been at a live music venue. maybe the lights made everyone think the band was singing directly to them. maybe the performers couldn't even see the audience. maybe they could.

although sabe appeared to be in his late thirties, he'd been on earth for much longer than that. in the old days, when only the anishinaabeg were here, he had a different name, a gentler, kinder name. he lived among them, but he rarely revealed himself. his job in those days was like his job now, he looked after people who had gotten lost, both physically and metaphorically. his inner nature was so sweet and gentle. his fur so soft. his strength so quiet. he walked with the anishinaabeg to teach them about both sides of honesty. the power of being forthcoming with another being and the art of cherishing another's most naked truth.

now things were different. sasquatch. bigfoot. yeti. sightings, like he was a ufo.

she waited for him after he'd finished playing. past last call, past the crowd of fans surrounding him as he tried to make it to the bar to get the last two of his free beers. the roadies started packing. the rest of the band headed for the van, to relax and get high. he patiently spoke to every fan, thanking each one of them with a mixture of humility, genuine surprise and embarrassment that only growing up in northern manitoba can instill in a person for the rest of their lives, and then he quietly sat down on the bar stool next to hers.

"hey."

"hey," she responded, meeting his eyes and then dropping hers to the floor.

"thanks for coming. sorry it was an off night for us."

"it was lovely," she answered, "lovely."

"ah thanks, thank you. that's really nice. i'm still sorry, i dunno know what happened."

what happened next is the kind of rare that happens only when certainty melts fear into nothingness. their eyes met and no one looked away. relief and breath poured into the space between their bodies. she pulled his body into hers, into an embrace of complete knowing, of profound acceptance. he let go of everything that he had to carry and fell into her arms. he had recognized her immediately.

although sabe appeared to be in her late thirties, she'd been on earth for much longer than that. in the old days, when only the nishnaabeg were here, she had a different name, a gentler, kinder name. she lived among them, but she rarely revealed herself. her job in those days, was like her job now, she looked after people who had gotten lost, both physically and metaphorically. her inner nature was so sweet and gentle. her fur so soft. her strength so quiet. she walked with the nishnaabeg to teach them about both sides of honesty. the power of being forthcoming with another being and the art of cherishing another's most naked truth.

now things were different. sasquatch. bigfoot. yeti. sightings, like she was a ufo.

they sat together, each unable to see themselves fully, but basking in the power of the other. they talked. about how hard it had become, and about how easy it had been in the coniferous trees of the north compared to the concrete of the cities, back when they didn't even know it was easy. they talked about the loneliness of their lives, so commonplace now, that each hardly noticed. they talked about the last time they had run into one of their own.

when they finished their beer, he asked if she would walk with him. they left the bar and headed west towards the river, the one that bubbles like a beating heart. they walked beside each other, feeling the energy of the other resonating, but being careful not to touch or brush arms. why, neither of them were sure. when they got to the river he put his arm around her and gently circled her forehead with his finger as if to mark her with his affection. a tear fell from her eye, hitting the ground like a heart beat. she told him 10 000 years of everything. they held each other.

the light of their nokomis rose and then cascaded down on the river of water spreading out before them. she bathed them in her warmth and watched over them as they kissed, as their love echoed out from the riverbank in concentric circles. a nighthawk flew over the water, diving through time and space head first towards the river with the full force of everything. two metres from the water and at the bottom of her dive, she flexed her wings upward. air rushed through her wingtips making a thunderous sound.

----

nishnaabemowin: sabe is big foot.

spacing

the distance between
ziigwan and mnokimaa
is the difference between
singing and not singing

broad leaves are born
we relearn fragile green
waves of wind
light harvested into food
sun making breath
river washing land
lake suffocating ice
trees bleeding sweet

i've only ever seen you
hitchhiking into dreams
or running from the headlights
but today
here you are
just sleeping. sitting. eating
hours of still
armfuls of nothing

and baapaase, fearless forest pilot
fast navigating, surgical maneuvering
unfolding red for the future
black for the past
white for the exactly right now

> *and you with your fortress of nice, trying to find something
> real, hiding in poetics, singing in hieroglyphics, moving around
> my flesh in semiotics, but never reaching out*

this distance is longer than all of our lives
we go, but different
bodies return
if they return at all.

---

nishnaabemowin: ziigwan is early spring when the snow is melting, mnokimaa is later spring and begins the moment the spring peepers start to sing, baapaase is a woodpecker.

it takes an ocean
not to break

i *knew you were going to try and kill yourself before you did it. i knew because before all this happened you were the only person my seven-year-old nephew with asperger's ever let hug him. you were eighteen and you were just shining, your even brown perfect skin competing with the bright blue sky for my attention. god, you were perfect. i was in love with the idea that finally we had given birth to a generation that didn't have to spend their adult lives recovering from their childhoods. you weren't going to drown yourself in anything. you were just going to smile and fight in some mythological honourable way we'd all only imagined. then i found out your mama was about to die and every time you looked me in the eye i wanted to cry, because i knew there was a diagnosed train wreck coming your way and i didn't know how someone so perfect could survive.*

after the accident we had the same three-line conversation for a month. therapy-lady suggested that it was insane for me to keep doing this with you, but fuck. i wasn't in therapy to take therapy-lady's advice. at least not all of it. i was there because i didn't want to fuck up my kids. that's not true. i was there so i didn't commit suicide.

it was too much to ask of a white lady.

after we stopped having the same three-line conversation over and over again you started to apologize to everyone for putting us through your accident. then you'd forget you apologized, and so a few hours later, you would do it all over again. it wasn't you talking, it was your team of therapists as they tried to get you to accept responsibility for your "bad choices" and the completely hellish reality those "choices" delivered you to.

therapy-lady was helping me "knit positive experiences into the fabric of my life." that sounded like unattainable crazy talk to me, but i liked that she said *fabric.* everyone else i knew said material.

bringing up trauma from my life made therapy-lady cry, especially if it was "aboriginal" themed. she said "aboriginal" a lot, and i knew she was trying to be respectful so i planned on letting it slide until the breaking point and then i was going to let her have it in one spiraling long manifesto. therapy-lady liked to compare my life to refugees from war-torn countries who hid their kids in closets when airplanes flew over their houses. this was her limit of understanding on colonized intimacy. she wasn't completely wrong, and while she tried to convince me none of us had to hide our kids anymore, we both knew that wasn't exactly true. i knew what every ndn knows: that vulnerability, forgiveness and acceptance were privileges. she made the assumption of a white person: they were readily available to all like the fresh produce at the grocery store.

lucy says that i made a critical mistake on my first day of therapy. "you have to lay all of your indian shit out on the first day, drug abuse, suicide attempts, all the times you got beat up, all of that shit. then you sit back and watch how they react. then you'll know if they can deal or not." lucy had a social work degree but she didn't buy it, which is always useful.

i wondered if these people had ever even thought of driving their car off a bridge? had they ever felt an overwhelming need for release? had they ever experienced the kind of pain that makes bad choices utterly rational? suicide's not something you do to other people, it's something you do for yourself.

i told you to stop apologizing. i told you it wasn't your fault. fuck sakes. i told you that you were in an enormous amount of pain. i told you that you were the fucking strongest person i'd ever known. i told you i knew why you did it.

lucy was right. but now i was two years invested in therapy-lady and plus i liked to interview therapy-lady about happy people like i was an anthropologist. apparently happy people celebrate their birthdays. apparently happy people express their emotions as a way of processing experiences. apparently the ability to throw yourself in front of a bus and not get that hurt isn't something happy people strive for.

if you're nish and you can't survive being dragged under the bus, you're not going to survive. period.

i want to suck the shame out of all forty-three of your broken bones.

i worried therapy-lady was trying to assimilate me into a plasticy christian that can stand in the middle of a car wreck and thank the heavenly father for the band aid they found in their purse. so while therapy-lady was crocheting my life of happy moments into a big fucking smothering scarf, i was imagining the release of ending it all. i was imagining floating away from the weight.

you apologized to me every day for another thirty days.

therapy-lady wanted me to tell her what i was getting out of these thirty-day conversations.

"intimacy."

"that's intensity, not intimacy. do you know the difference?"

"probably not."

i try again.

i decide she can't possibly ever get it.

when it first happened, everyone was praying for you to live. i wanted to trust you. you saw what was laid out before you and you made a choice.

shit. that's not what i'm supposed to say. i'm supposed to say i'm glad you're alive. i'm glad it didn't work. i'm supposed to look you in the eye and tell you that it's all going to be better, and when you don't believe me, i'm supposed to tell you to trust me. the mother in me has to be the beacon of your future ok self that tells you unequivocally not to trust your feelings because they will pass. what's that crap that therapy-lady says? "the feelings are real, but they are not reality." yeah. that's it. your feelings are real, but they are not your reality. don't get tricked.

the mother in me has to believe i can heal you by loving you, because no one actually believes that, except for mothers.

fuck. why was the universe trying to destroy you? why didn't you get some say? sometimes people's lives are just shit through no fault of their own and not even fucking oprah's cash and her tool box of privileged platitudes can fix it. sometimes people just drown in their own heads for no particular reason. sometimes people are just sad. you know, if it had worked, i would still have respected you. i would have respected your decision, and i would have missed you and loved you the same as i do now.

but it didn't work and now you're in this mess, with all the shit that got you to this point in the first place and all the new shit of being shattered pieces of skin arced over the pavement. i'm scared for the point where you heal enough to see how monumentally bad this is.

she asks me again, "what's in it for you?"

i think about stealing her desk.

i give another incorrect answer.

"again, what is in it for you?"

"love."

"love?"

"love. and that is all."

i change the subject to anxiety. therapy-lady loves talking about anxiety. me the poor depressed indian. her the white fucking pathologizing saviour. i tell her my anxiety and i are co-dependent, but in a lovely way. she tries to convince me the world is a safe place, and that i'm not a little kid anymore and that it's possible that no one will ever hit me again. sometimes when she says things like that, it's like i've never heard them before and so i ask if i can borrow her pen, so i write them down on my hand. and then i go back to worrying that my jeans are too dirty for her white ikea couch, and that maybe i'll leave a big grey stain of me on it.

i'm getting in the car right now, and i'm driving north to you. it'll take me a couple of days to get there. i want to pick you up, and i'm going to stitch every one of your broken bones back together with kisses, and then i'm going to drive us to the coast. i'm not sure which one. but i like the feeling of listening to music and driving and driving for days to get to somewhere different.

i think you're going to like that feeling too.

buffalo on

round 1

*r*ight off the bat, let's just admit we're both from places that have been fucked up through no fault of our own in a thousand different ways for seven different generations and that takes a toll on how we treat each other. it just does.

we're all hunting around for acceptance, intimacy, connection and love, but we don't know what those particular med'cines even look like so we're just hunting anyway with vague ideas from dreams and hope and intention, at the same time dragging around blockades full of reminders that being vulnerable has never ended well for any of us, not even one single time.

there are some things you can escape and there are some things you cannot.

still, i know us, and i know we're going to fight like hell to escape, and sometimes we will and sometimes we won't and at some point we won't know what we've lost or what we're trying to gain, but that's why i'm here to remind you: it's acceptance, intimacy, connection and love. that's it. that's all we're looking for. and you can't have a single one of those things even for a second if your dead. so that is item number one: make sure you're alive. make sure you survive. make sure you are not dead.

second of all, the skill set you need to survive is not the same skill set you need to love and be loved. and while all those white mothers were holding their babies and stroking their heads and singing them songs, i'd like to say all our brown mamas were doing the same but they weren't often afforded the luxury. yes. luxury. they were targeted and they knew we'd be targeted.

thirdly, they are going to berate you, attack you, shame you and worse. they are going to rape you and beat you and no one's going to be there to save you. so you better know how to save yourself. you better know how to get the fuck up. you better know how to pick up pieces and move on. you better know how to quit feeling sorry for yourself and pull up your socks.

chin up.
buck up.
shut up.

you better not whine and cry and act like the world is going to end because it isn't. you're not the first person to go through this. it was way worse for the kids locked in the basement of that residential school with no food and no water for days on end. it was way worse for those kids when those priests invented their own makeshift electric chair. remember that. it was worse for those kids whose parents were kidnapped and locked away in iron lungs until it didn't matter anymore. you don't even know how lucky you are.

it's the way it is. it is what it is. it's bound to happen and when it does you are going to *buffalo* on.

when you come out, come out swinging.

that's how kwe's mom raised her. that's how my mom raised me. that's how all the mom's raised all the hers. when you're raising someone to survive a war that the other side invests millions in convincing people it doesn't exist, you raise your army to be tough. you teach them not to make a big fuss. you teach them to not feel. if you waste your time feeling, you're not going to be ready and in the ring for the next blow. you're going to be crying and feeling sorry for yourself in the corner and you're not going to see him coming. because that's the lesson: you never see them coming.

kwe's mom taught her how to do everything because she'd need to know how to do everything. chop wood. light a fire. light your inner fire. keep it lit. blow on the embers. fan the flames. fire needs breath. life needs fire. breath feeds shkode.

her mom did not teach her how to accept a lover's caress, a kind word or a helping hand. so instead we did shots of jameson and fucked every friday night in a bathroom stall in bar down the road by a lake, not too far from here.

that's how we were gentle.

round 2

after 89 years of eating squirrel, muskrat, groundhog and tomato macaroni wiener soup, my hunting and fishing rights have arrived back at the pleasure of the crown. the letter said as of october 29, you can hunt and fish the 1818 treaty area and please do not flaunt your rights in front of the ontario federation of hunters and anglers.

so me and my best kwe drove down to the ofha headquarters, set up our lawn chairs, built a bit of a shkode and nailed two signs into the ground that read: first we'll kill your animals and fish, then we'll fuck your wives (with their consent, of course). we stayed there for two days, until the cops came and told us we were tres-passing and no one knew what our signs meant anyway. you cannot apparently write "fuck" on a sign in public and then just sit beside it smoking electronic cigarettes because we're trying to quit and eating sandwiches out of the cooler. you cannot just protest for no reason, you have to have some reason and come on, you're making your people look bad. they didn't send the regular cops though. they drove out and got the rez cop, and sent him over to talk us down. which i guess is an improvement because sometimes they just shoot. so garry comes over and is all "what's all this?" acting cop-like, and we're biting the insides of our cheeks saying "aaniin gookoosh," and garry's biting the insides of his cheeks too because we just learned that particular farm animal all together in language class on wednesday. then kwe says, "what the fuck took you so long? we've been here for two days, we're starting to run out of goddamn sandwiches." garry says we have to be gone by tomorrow or there's going to be charges.

so i leave ofha headquarters early, and i therefore get home early and i open the bedroom door and there's garry all missionary, pumping his shit stick into some 25-year-old college zhaganashi-kwe. i feel embarrassed for garry when our eyes meet. and yes, i feel contempt when my eyes meet hers imagining how impressive garry must seem when you can't see through his veneer and when you don't know enough to see he stopped self actualizing in 1998. when you can only see wild exotic savage lover.

his weakness is all splayed out before me in a lake and i can see 15 m to the bottom. it burns—the idea that me and her and her vacuous 25-year-old mind are equivalent.

"sorry."

"sorry for what?"

"i'm sorry you had to see that."

"me too."

"it doesn't mean anything."

"fuck who you want."

"you don't understand."

"i understand. i don't care who you fuck."

"you're just saying that because you're mad."

"i'm just saying that because i love you but i don't care who else you fuck."

"now what?"

"now what, what?"

"well i don't know what happens next."

"of course you don't."

"of course i don't?"

"of course you don't."

"you're sitting there, expecting me to freak, expecting me to be mad and cry and throw random objects at you and call you a loser and selfish and a cheater. and you're all ready to defend yourself and tell me it means nothing and tell me she means nothing and that it will never happen again. and that's all bullshit. you're trying to fill the gaping hole. white pussy filled it for ten minutes. now you're in the exact same position you were in this morning with your gaping hole. nothing's changed."

"no nothing's changed."

"fine."

round 3

kwe and i are at the burial mounds because we decided to start using them as graves again and her kookum gets to the sharing part of the ceremony and she tells the person to her left to share some words and then it will be the next person's turn, and at the end we will do the double hug circle and everyone will go home.

so my turn is coming down the path faster than i'd like and just
before it's my turn, i remember this:

*auntie and uncle were fighting over whose turn it is to wear the big gold
elephant necklace and auntie's wearing white pants and stiletto heels
even though we're camping in a white people park and her heels keep
sinking in the muddy grass but it doesn't stop her from looking classy
on her lawn chair by the shkode.*

*there were burial mounds just past those cedars over there and i hope
those dead ones can't hear us. it's may 24th weekend and you say it
two-four, not twenty-four. there isn't supposed to be any drinking in the
park, so the bottles have to be hidden in the tent. there isn't supposed
to be any indians in the park either, but don't worry, we don't even
know we are indians yet.*

*the old man is at the fire and it's getting dark and he's too tired to get
up and get his own drink so he sends me into the tent and he tells me
to mix one for the old lady too. i'm eight. i don't know too much about
mixing drinks, but i know that you get into shit if you make them too
weak. so i pour mostly rye into the plastic yellow cup and only a little
bit of ginger ale, just to be on the safe side.*

that'll put hair on your chest.

holay shit. she mixes drinks like the old lady.

*they've been drinking all day and with that last drink he's drunk, but
he's a happy drunk, and now she's drunk too and she's happy now, but
she'll turn. just wait, she'll turn.*

*she turns. one minute she's sitting on her lawn chair, the next, she's
sitting cross legged by the fire. she's war whooping. she's drumming her
hands on the ground in war beats. she's singing ten little indians and
doing the rain dance. then she's powwow dancing with maniacal speed
and screaming we're indians! we're indians! we're all indians! over and
over. and then finally, after the bloody crescendo finally runs out, a
simple "the reserve is right over there."*

*mom takes me to the tent, and she gets me ready for bed. i brush my
teeth without water and spit onto the ground. i change into damp
pajamas. i change into skin dripping dirty drops of shame and fear.*

"is it true, we're indians?"

"no. grandma's just drunk."

memory searing skin.
ancestors marking warriors.
land giving up truths.
skin made of someone else's shame.

only drunks and children and ancestors tell the truth.

that's it.

round 4

she's telling me tomorrow is the day she is going to die and i believe
her. her eighty-four-year-old body has twenty-four more hours of
breath left inside and that's it. i always think that old people are
different than me, and looking into her land-coloured eyes right
now, i know that's crap. she and i are exactly the same. i'm going
to be eighty-four and i'm not going to feel any different than i do
right now. i'm not going to be wise or brave or all-knowing. i'm
just going to be old inhabiting a body on the precipice of betraying
me forever. the suicide of everything.

"what do you want to do old woman?"

"i want to go swimming."

"in the lake?"

"in the lake."

"at night."

"tonight?"

"it's the only night left."

"it is."

"i can't believe it's over."

"yeah, this part is almost over. it sucks."

"i want to do something fun."

"fun, hey?"

"nanabush, i want to kiss you."

"ha. no, you don't."

"yes i do."

"fifty years ago, maybe."

"no, now."

"it's because you pity me."

"it's because i love you."

"not like that."

"not like what?"

"i don't want to die a dirty old man."

"you're dying a dirty old man already, or i guess right now, you're a dirty old woman."

"ha."

"ha."

"if we'd been born the same year, we'd have already kissed."

"and more."

"and more."

"so fuck time."

"i don't know."

"i think you've got skills."

"i think you've got standards."

"i don't want to die a fool."

"we all die as fools."

"death as humility."

"death as humiliation."

"death as transformation."

"death as transportation."

"it will be the only thing you'll remember about me."

"if you're good."

"i'm good."

"it's not all i'll remember."

"we shouldn't have talked about it."

"no, we shouldn't have talked about it."

"shut up. i'm doing it."

kwe picks me up the next day after the family's been called. it's just starting to snow but i can't tell if it is serious yet. the brown of the land has been covered with light. kwe doesn't talk, knowing there is nothing she can say that will make a bit of difference.

my bones, a heap in the passenger seat.

ishpadinaa

*i*f i write in small characters no one will notice my grandma's lying on a picnic table in dufferin grove park.

aanikoobijigan: ancestor
aanikoobijigan: great grand child
aanikoobijigan: great grand mother

the sign in the park says: when an indian dies on a picnic table in downtown toronto, call 911.

do not touch me. do not call 911. and get that fucking look off of your face.

people keep stopping and asking if we want help. like dads with jobs and espresso and buggies and couples with indoor scarves, sick in love. it's because no one is calling 911. they are trying to be nice because the scene doesn't make sense.

she says to me "i got really smart by reading every book in the rockton library, or maybe you don't think i am so smart, little miss phd."

i tell myself that this is a good place to die, even though there are hotdogs and cake and balloons. it's outside. there are no fluorescent lights. there's no one trying to fix the damage that can't be fixed. she doesn't want death to be like a math test, i tell myself.

she says to me "all husbands are boring, so pick one that lets you do whatever you want."

i notice her fetal skeleton underneath ironed polyester dress pants. the loving family is locked in a telephone booth of rising anxiety. we are stretching our necks out to take the last sips of air.

she says to me "if you don't have 7up you can mix vodka with beer."

the kids are digging large holes in the sand and then placing driftwood across the holes to make bridges. i don't know where they got the driftwood, it's downtown toronto, but i'm glad they are not paying any attention.

she says to me "you work too hard, you'll never be happy."

aanikoobijigan: to tie together, a bond, a link
aanikoobijigan: my broken paper chain from when i was six
aanikoobijigan: to measure loss

---

nishnaabemowin: ishpadinaa means a hill.

96

caged

*g*idigaa bizhiw paced back and forth in her cage. it helped pass the time. it helped create a rhythm that distracted her from the kids in strollers and the cameras and the irritating parents that came to see her. none of them ever did, see her, that is. not in a real way, not in a way that saw her person. in fact, she wondered if it was actually still possible to be seen.

a lot of animals adapt to being in the zoo. they adapt to the rhythm of feeding, cleaning, being on display. they forget where they came from. they forget the feeling of running fast and free and until their legs feel like exploding. they forget the exhilaration of the chase, the deep pathos of the kill. they forget the breath that space provides, and then their children forget. it is easier that way. but gidigaa bizhiw remembered. she remembered intensely, with her full body, and it ached. she ached. she lived with the pain of discon-nection, she coveted it, and she learned from it, as all warriors do. sometimes she would allow herself to drown in it, coming up only for desperate gasps of air. she believed with her heart that this place held the map back, answers to finding the way out. she believed that each day she hung on, she was closer to glimpsing that map. each night provided another opportunity for her soul to vision the map into existence. during the night she paced. when dawn presented an opportunity she slipped out, her body sleeping through the day, her soul traveling. when dusk called the two back together, she began her methodical laps around her cage. back and forth, back and forth, until the dirt was worn. she waited.

to an outsider, it might look like gidigaa bizhiw was drowning. unable to adapt, unable to live, able only to pace. but most people couldn't see the strategist in her. her pacing was less coping than a deliberate act to liberate her soul from her body, so she could bask more fully in the vision of her ancestors. it was her ceremony. it was the way that she slipped through this reality into the other world. she could travel into day through the forests of maple or white pine, the lakes, nanabush's rocks. walking and then running. running then walking. she sat with her mother. she drank from the river. she breathed.

in the times between her traveling, she relied on similar pleasures, pleasures no one could take away from her. solitary pleasure. the way the sky looked, its anticipatory colour just before the first rays of sun rose each day. the sound of the wind just before it changed. the taste of rain in mid summer.

traveling was never easy to accomplish. it was as much a finely crafted skill as it was a raw ability. she had been taught. she had practiced her craft. and while the other animals met her elusive solitude, her gentleness and her willing vulnerability with fear and suspicion, there was one that was different. the one that was the great healer. that one, was different.

each day was the same in the zoo. nothing ever happened. nothing ever changed.

until it of course, it did.

naabak was moved into the exhibit across from gidigaa bizhiw in spring. it was temporary, when the time was right, he would be moved in with the female bear, in an arranged marriage or perhaps a marriage of convenience. naabak was weak when he arrived. gidigaa bizhiw could see that. his normally warm red light was barely even visible from his cage. he was tired, drained, injured.

out of the corner of her eye, naabak tried to catch her attention. but gidigaa bizhiw was pacing. always pacing. focused strategy. quiet strength. finally, after several days, naabak rallied enough strength to lumber over to the side of the cage closest to gidigaa bizhiw. he collapsed in a heap and watched. naabak waited for an opportunity to catch her eye. but gidigaa bizhiw paced all night, slept all day. she never looked up. there was never a chance, she made sure of that.

gidigaa bizhiw continued to pace around the outside edge of her cage in a circular motion following the pattern of the sun. after several laps her senses became muted, her consciousness slowing to reset itself. the sounds left into the background. her body became loose, more detached from her soul than normal. her eyes blurred into the slate grey of the chain link fence. she focused intensely knowing that if the doorway opened, her soul could jump through if it was liberated enough from her physicality.

today was a rhythm like any other. but today, rather than the monochrome of the slate grey gidigaa bizhiw normally saw out of the corner of her eye, she saw a flash of red light. she stopped. she looked up. her eyes met his. immediately she saw the intense, warm red light surrounding his body. the light radiating outwards from his black fur. it was an energy that pulled her in. held onto her. sucked every bit of tension, of hurt, of weight out of her body, until she was able to slip out of her cage and collapse into his arms. he barely touched his paw to the tip of her spine, moving slowly down, each vertebrae relaxing into the next. her back stretched in length as the angst she didn't know she carried left the boney scaffolding that held her up. surrounded in the safest of ways, his breath warmed the base of her neck, her cool green simultaneously engulfing and being engulfed by his red. this one could see her. she could still be seen by this one.

animals know that their strategists live in the bad. it's their responsibility. protection is the weight they carry. protection is bizhiw's sacrifice. she thinks ahead, she plans for the worst-case scenarios. she worries. she watches. she thinks, and she does it alone. bears are also solitary, but they are healers. they take the negative away. they cleanse. they calm the pain and they invigorate the heart. they restore the balance. they lead with their hearts, must have healing, because it is the sustenance of peace. they carry the burden of peace.

gidigaa bizhiw got comfortable with the red energy. she got comfortable with the good, the weightlessness. traveling was easier. she had to pace much less to achieve liberation. naabak was making everything easier. she watched as spring faded into summer. it wouldn't be long now. she knew it wouldn't be long now.

she wasn't surprised when one day she got back from traveling and he was gone. the exhibit was empty. good strategists are never surprised. the birds gathered and sang that he had been moved in with nozhem. they reported that the connection was spectacular. nozhem's purple had fused with his red. and the creation was a thing of such beauty that sky world had chosen to recreate it at dawn and at dusk as a retelling of the beauty. there would be cubs.

gidigaa bizhiw went back to pacing. she felt numb, full of anxiety, like she needed to run, but she knew she couldn't travel in that state. the doorway wouldn't open. she was trapped. she considered that maybe the ancestors gave her a gift. she considered that maybe they didn't—that tasting that bear had only made everything that much worse. most gifts were like that, which was why she rarely accepted them.

she sat with her disappointment. she was disappointed in herself for allowing this. for giving so freely of herself. she was disappointed in naabak for his complete and utter surrender to nozhem. his amnesia of their connection. she wished she had clawed him in a desperate attempt to transfer to him some of the pain she felt. to mark him, in a way he had marked her. she avoided dusk and dawn and the remembrance. she sat inside the loss. she paced. she tried to travel. she paced in order to travel.

each day was the same in zoo. nothing ever happened. nothing ever changed.

until, of course, it did.

one evening in late summer, gidigaa bizhiw was pacing in her cage preparing for a night of traveling. usually the slate grey of the chain link fence blurred in the corner of her eye as she walked past. but this evening, the grey was intersected by warm red. he was back. intense warm red light surrounded his body and then hers. radiating outwards from his black fur and her brown spotted coat. it was an energy that pulled her in. held onto her. sucked every bit of tension, of hurt, of weight out of her body, until she was able to slip out of her cage and collapse into his arms. he barely touched his paw to the tip of her spine, moving slowly down, each vertebra relaxing into the next. her back stretched in length as the angst she didn't know she carried left the rusted scaffolding that held her up. surrounded in the safest of ways, his breath warmed the base of her neck, her cool green simultaneously engulfing and being engulfed by his red. this one could see her. she could still be seen by this one.

when she was light enough to fly, she left the cage and engaged in her daily travels. her search for life outside of the cage was becoming much more urgent. the winds were shifting, but she was finding only pieces of the map, not the full map. she collected the pieces, focused on them, dreamed about them, traveled with them, hoping that the other clans had found pieces too. then, when they got out of their cages, they could dance those pieces into existence. when she got back in the evening, she entered her body asleep on the cedar platform and at nightfall she resumed her pacing.

he came infrequently, but persistently. over time she learned to sense his vulnerability, his want, like the intensity of too young thunderbirds flying over the land in mid summer. today, he sat outside her cage and gently poked his fingers through the bars at the bottom of the cage, touching the tip of her paw. his humidity felt heavy on her body even though they were barely touching. breathing him in was a weight, and taking that heaviness inside of her dampened the lightness of her green. in automatic response the green recoiled inward, pulling her closer, smiling, laughing even, leaving no holes to be filled. this time she would be the one to leave and in that moment they both knew it. so naabak rolled up his piece of the map, and pushed it through the bars of her enclosure. gidigaa bizhiw took it, surprised she never considered that he might be a piece of her puzzle.

by the next full moon, the cage began to fade. ever so slightly at first, and then gathering momentum as its departure became more committed. particle by particle it disappeared, such that the zoo-keepers didn't notice until it was too late. even gidigaa bizhiw didn't notice at first. but after a while, out of the corner of her eye, just before she paced her way into the other world, the slate grey seemed less intense, its permanence called into question. it was fading. in time, the structure would become weakened, so that at the right time she could slip through it to the other world, this time taking her body with her. the time was near when her research would be complete. where the cage would fade completely into the landscape and she'd have to live in a different world in a different way.

gidigaa bizhiw is a strategist and a warrior. the strategist sits with the pain. or maybe she sits beside the pain. maybe the warrior, the one that carries the burden of peace also carries the burden of love—of embracing connection in the face of utter disconnection. maybe there is no limit on love.

nishnaabemowin: gidigaa bizhiw is a spotted lynx or bobcat, naabak is a male bear, nozhem is a female bear spirit.

gezhizhwazh

*e*veryone always tells wiindigo stories when they should be telling gezhizhwazh stories. that's what this old one says.

"why you telling wiindigo stories all the time?"

"maybe because they're about greed and evil and imbalance and we're all living surrounded by that."

"well then why you want to be surrounded by more of that?"

"i dunno. so we see the wiindigo in ourselves?"

"gaa. you young ones forget everything nowadays. wiindigo more about the inside than the outside."

"so what should we be telling then?"

"you know."

"i don't think i do, know, that is."

"*tell the ones about that strong young nishnaabekwe who wasn't afraid of those wiindigo. who was smart and strategic. who was patient, so, so patient. waiting until just the right time. waiting, watching. tell those ones, so those young ones will know what to do. teach those ones. make it so they'll want to listen. make it so they'll pay attention.*"

"*like a movie?*"

"*gaawin! not like a movie. everything got to be a movie with this generation. everything got to be 'an app.' not a movie, that one. a story. i show you. your job is to listen.*"

this one came into the world a fast-moving cloud gliding through the doorway like she was riding the southwind and by the time i met her, she was tens of thousands of years old. you wouldn't know it to see her though. she was thin and muscular, but not overly so, not like she spent all her time in the gym. her long black hair was very straight. her skin olive, her eyes a dark, haunting brown. her hair was almost always in a ponytail or a single braid mirroring her spine. she was good at transforming too, that one. one minute she was turning heads she was so sexy, and the next minutes she was walking through the crowd unnoticed.

"*do you really think we should be talking about sexy in the middle of this not-a-wiindigo-story, auntie?*"

"*why not? when'd sexy get so bad to talk about? you wouldn't even be here without sexy. sexy got you here. no, no, no we're talking about sexy. we all sexy. sexy make the world go round.*"

"*auntie. i don't want to hear old people talk about sex.*"

"*what you got against old people talking about sex? you think we not got sexy anymore? you think i didn't have my share of husbands and lovers? you think sexy expires?*"

"*um, no, i guess not. i just don't want to hear the details.*"

"*hear the details? you lucky if i tell you the details! i'm the old lady story teller and if i want to put sexy in my story, sexy is in my story. you the listener and your job is to listen. here we go.*"

it wasn't easy for her. a lot of people had been made to forget. when they did remember, they remembered him, not her. the teacher. the one that taught by never learning. the one that had pissed off every aspect of creation at some point. the only reason everyone seemed to remember him and not her was because of his shameless self-promotion. it was brilliant of him really, as the teacher he was supposed to reflect back the worst of what had happened, and it used to work. people used to get it.

but for her, this version of him made him a self-centred, egotistical pain in the ass. but when they were alone, it was effortless and she'd come to rely on them more than she should, given that the situation they were now in was utterly unreliable by nature.

"whoa auntie, i think maybe you going too far with the sexy now. you don't want to piss, you know, those guys off. some of them ones like to keep it clean, on the up and up. i don't know about you making all these stories pornographic …"

"howah. when did sex get pornographic? who said anything about pornographic? your thinking is all messed up, boy. not all sexy is pornographic. sexy not suppose to be pornographic. hola. i need to get some money from inac to give your generation sexy lessons."

"well why you using all this big words anyway? why you not talking normal? and where is your rez accent? why aren't you talking like an indian?"

"howah. i'll show you my rez accent. not everyone like my accent. not everyone listen when i talk in my accent. some people only think that i'm smart when i talk like peter mansbridge. it's about audience. some audiences you got to lose your accent and use big english words. you think i can't use big english words? i'll show you. none of that stuff is important anyway. what is important is who is listening."

"i dunno, i think it is more authentic if you speak rez, auntie. it's more decolonized."

"what do you know about decolonized? you think sexy is pornographic. you think i can't use five dollar words. you think i'm only authentic if i'm talking rez. you the one suppose to be listening anyway. how can you be doing any listening when you're all critical about my authenti-ci-ty?

the two of them were both travelers, but they never traveled together. he traveled from place to place visiting. checking reality. testing reality. shaking hands, being everywhere at once but still nowhere. telling stories, helping. always helping that guy, even when it made everything much worse. she was also always in motion, but in the background. she solved problems ahead of time, as a negotiator, a strategist, a quiet protector who no one saw. she'd saved his ass more times than she could count.

"what? you not going to interrupt me and ask about 'ass?'"

"no. you told me to sit quietly ... but yes, i think you should change 'ass' to 'life.'"

"oh you do, do you? look at you, the big shot, editing my story. howah, you're showing signs of zhaganashiiyaadizi. you're a worry alright. but right now, the show must go on."

there was a certain amount of loneliness that came with living through the centuries and the times she hooked up with him helped with that. or at least that's what she told herself. he seemed to be able to see her as only one of her own kind could, but at other times, he switched that off entirely, getting lost in the intensity that he carried with him like his own personal whirlwind.

gezhizhwazh, as she was now called, was well known to only the oldest anishinaabeg, as the one that had rather dramatically defeated the wiindigo. many generations ago, she'd planned and carried out a successful resistance against the wiindigo by sacrificing herself. not just a successful resistance, but the successful resistance. they ate her slowly, as they planned an attack on a small anishinaabeg village. she endured, persisted, sacrificed. she learned their plans. she studied them. she learned to think like them. she gained their respect and trust and led them into the village. it was then that her strength of heart rose to the surface and she betrayed her enemy. she told the anishinaabeg of their plan. taught them how to kill wiindigo, and the wiindigo were defeated. and once she did, those old ones say she cut off their balls. it was the greatest defeat in the history of the world, and for a while at least, everyone had remembered. everyone had celebrated.

"how come i never heard about no defeat."

"i dunno. how come you not heard of a lot of things?"

but by now, the anishinaabeg had lived without the wiindigo for so long, or so they'd thought, that they'd relegated wiindigo out of real life and into the realm of myth. they'd forgotten entirely that story and reality are one and the same. a critical mistake because the wiindigo had insidiously reincarnated and come back stronger. instead of an insatiable appetite for the anishinaabeg, this time, they had had an insatiable appetite for anishinaabeg aki and all of its gifts. of course, to the anishinaabeg this was the same thing.

this seemingly minor adjustment in wiindigo strategy had shored up their superior military power and made death for the anishinaabeg much slower and more painful than before and any potential interventions were that much more difficult to realize. wiindigo had diffused their political power since the old days, their system of replication had become more complex and they'd hired public relations experts. hell, they'd invented public relations experts. their system of replication permeated everything. they were brilliant instead of just scary, and they found a way to convince people to buy disconnection, insatiable hunger and emptiness. the lucky ones worked their whole lives so they could buy more disconnection, hunger and emptiness. the unlucky ones were destroyed by it, and the unluckier still had parents that were destroyed by it. the more people that ate their own young, the stronger the wiindigo got.

for gezhizhwazh it had become difficult to know where to intervene. things had become so fucked up. the last years she'd spent being a sex worker to the elite of bay street. before that, she'd been a linesman for hydro, a political aide, a nuclear engineer at the bruce, a bureaucrat. she'd deciphered the system. she could think like them. she mimicked them. she'd diagnosed the problem. but this time, the betrayal was more complicated—a search for meaning in a vast sea of contradictions. she won battle after battle after battle, with virtually no impact on wiindigo power. what was she missing? it seemed so much simpler last time. she called on the other guy.

"i don't get it. i can see them. i know them. i can think like them while still thinking like me, but nothing i do stops them. nothing i do disrupts it."

"then you're not thinking like them," he replied as he ran his big toe slowly up the inside of her leg.

"i *am* thinking like them, so much so, i sometimes forget i'm me. it's not that," she said.

"then what is it gezh?" he asked nudging his nose into the space between her ear lobe and her neck.

"it's that this time their power is all over the place. there is no single target. it's everywhere."

"then start at the beginning, even everywhere starts at the beginning. fix the beginning, gezh, maybe the rest will follow."

gezhizhwazh rolled over facing her other one. that right there was why she loved him. he gently touched her forehead in soft lines, more like breath than touch. he wrapped his body around hers, and then slipped into sleep. she held onto her thoughts.

"how come you not interrupting me? my story no good? you asleep?"

"i thought it was disrespectful to interrupt."

"it is. but you're not interrupting is making me self-conscious, like my story is no good."

"the story's good auntie. keep going."

"ok. pay attention to this next part, it's important."

when gezhizhwazh needed to heal, and renew herself, she had learned to mother. the stability and rhythm of a new life filled her up. the constant physical contact. the love. the birth ceremony was renewal in itself. no wonder men had to work to not become lost. no wonder. but birth was the one ceremony that you still had to be careful with. the one that happens countless times every day in the world. wiindigo kept that one controlled through medical intervention for maternal health and of course the health of the baby. this translated into drugging women so they couldn't be present at their ceremony. planned c-sections. putting a plastic nipple in the baby instead of her own flesh. putting her in a plastic box instead of in the arms of a warm, living, breathing human.

gezhizhwazh knew this was how those wiindigo first planted the hole inside each of these new little people in the first place. the hole that they tried so desperately to fill for the rest of their lives. they filled it up with food, with drink, with stuff. they cut themselves down, flooded themselves, they fevered themselves. they ate, drank, swam and breathed in the toxic soup they'd inadvertently created, all in an attempt to fill the bottomless hole. they sat in front of screens for most of their waking hours. they became cannibals.

gezhizhwazh figured that part out. she'd figured out the next part too. that if she could bring new life through the doorway without that hole, there would be nothing to feed. without the weight of large gaping holes in their beings, people would no longer be willing to pay for disconnection. with nothing to feed, the entire system would fall apart. so while that other one was out carousing, protesting or pontificating to anyone who would listen, gezhizhwazh was at work as a bami ondaadiziike, circling around those birthing women to protect that ceremony. foiling those interventions, protecting the circle. for now, her battle with the wiindigo was in its resurgence stage. gezhizhwazh was building an army—a diffuse, scattered group of souls that could see through the wiindigo illusion, because they were whole.

the light of gezhizhwazh's army of dancing eyes would change the world.

just wait.

"just wait for what?"

"you just wait. that's it."

"that's it? nothing happened? it's a great set up, but ... but i don't know if you should be messing around with gezhizhwazh and wiindigo stories especially if nothing is going to happen."

"nothing happened? howah, you don't even know a story when you hear it. it doesn't all come to you at once. you can't just press a button and get all the answers. press the button, get all the answers, then what you going to do, big shot?"

"then what do we do?"

"you just wait, i already told you. and while you are waiting, get me some tea, and maybe something to eat. i'm hungry after all that story-telling."

---

nishnaabemowin: zhaganashiiyaadizi means to be colonized, live as a white person at the expense of being nishnaabe, gezhizhwazh means to cut.

nogojiwanong

she is the only doorway into this world

i. it is with great regret that we are writing on behalf of the michi saagiig anishinaabeg to inform you that you will not be permitted to build your lift locks, canals and hydro dams here because this is the place where we come to sit and talk with our aanikoobijiganag.

ii. it is with great regret that we are writing on behalf of the michi saagiig anishinaabeg to inform you that you will not be permitted to build your lift locks, canals and hydro dams because these are the rivers we use to travel from chi'nibiish to waasegamaa. these routes are vital to the health and well-being of our relatives, pimiziwag and maajaamegosag.

iii. it is with great regret that we are writing on behalf of the michi saagiig anishinaabeg that you will not be permitted to build your lift locks, canals and hydro dams because we cannot permit concrete shackles on our mother, she needs to be free to move around in order to cleanse and give birth.

iv. it is with great regret that we are writing on behalf of the michi saagiig anishinaabeg to inform you that you will not be permitted to build your lift locks, canals and hydro dams because the fish, eels, birds, insects, plants, turtles, and reptiles do not consent to the damage your project will cause.

v. it is with great regret that we are writing on behalf of the michi saagiig anishinaabeg to inform you will not be permitted to build your lift locks, canals and hydro dams because the caribou, elk, deer, bison, lynxes, foxes, wolves, wolverines, martens, otters, muskrats, bears, skunks, raccoons, beavers, squirrels and chipmunks do not consent to the damage your project will cause.

vi. it is with great regret that we are writing on behalf of the michi saagiig anishinaabeg to inform you that you will not be permitted to build your lift locks, canals and hydro dams because of the damage it will cause our sugar bushes and minomiin beds, and our relatives the ducks and geese that depend on those beds for food.

vii. it is with great regret that we are writing on behalf of the michi saagiig anishinaabeg to inform you will not be permitted to build your lift locks, canals and hydro dams here because this is the place where we give birth and breastfeed, and we like to drink the water while doing so. the clean water in our wombs and breasts is the same clean water in the rivers and lakes.

this is the place where we come to sit and talk with our aanikoobi-jiganag.

signed this 21st day of june, eighteen hundred and thirty, nogoji-wanong, kina gichi anishinaabeg-ogaming.

kaniganaa,

wenona x

gizhiikokwe x

niimkii binesikwe x

nokomis x

ogichidaakwe, jijaak doodem x

ogichidaakwe, migizi doodem x

ogichidaakwe, adik doodem x

nishnaabemowin: nogojiwanong is the mississauga name for peterborough and means the place at the foot of the rapids, michi saagiig nishnaabeg is the name for mississauga nishnaabeg people and means lives at the mouth of rivers, aanikobijiganag means ancestors, great-grandmothers, great-grandfathers, and great-grandchildren, literally "the links that bind us together" or a chain, chi'nibiish is the mississauga name for lake ontario, waasegamaa is the nishnaabeg name for georgian bay, maajaamegosag is a name for salmon, pimiziwag is a name for eels, minomiin is wild rice, kina gchi anishinaabeg-ogaming means the place where we all live and work together, wenona is a spirit-being whose name means "the first breast feeder," gizhiigokwe is sky-woman, nokomis is grandmother, nimkii binesikwe means thunderbird woman, ogichidaakwe is a holy woman, jijaak is crane, doodem is clan, migizi is bald eagle, adik is caribou, bald eagle and crane are clans associated with mississauga territory, kaniganaa is a word often spoken at the end of prayer or scared songs.

she asked why

yeah, it was me. i blew the fucking lift lock up in downtown peterborough and then tara wrote a song about it. so what. sue me. arrest me. i hated that thing and you should have hated it too, if you'd ever stopped to think about it critically, like even for a second, and so now parks canada has one less nationalism park in its collection of family jewels. big deal.

you know what? i tried something more reasonable. i fucking tried to paint it into the landscape like that artist dude in green grass, running water … or was it truth and bright water. i can't remember. ali knows. ask her. i tried to paint it into the landscape, but big surprise, it didn't work.

i don't know where you're going to fucking skate in the winter and i don't care. oh wait, skate on the lake. oh wait, it doesn't freeze anymore because you wrecked the weather. i don't know where the optimist club is going to hold its fishing derby and i don't care. oh wait, fish in the lake. oh wait, your cottages wrecked all the fish in the lake. i don't know where those big shots from toronto are going to drive their drunken yachts this summer, scoping out waterfront lots for their monster cottages.

maybe they can go bowling at bowl-a-rama instead.

she asked them for help

howah. when them binesiwag strike, it is with precision. they don't mess around those ones. no way. they strike and boom. the job is done.

oh but they full of it those young ones. can't be helped. so much energy flying up so high, darting back down. this one mama, they called her aanjibines. transformer that one, changer, renewer. she live high up on that mountain over there, and she taking care of two young ones. the boy's name was echo-maker. the girl's name was overseer. overseer just watched and listened while echo-maker flapped around, squawked and whined. she was strong footed, that one.

they lived up there, in a big, big nest, so they could watch over everything. nahow, when this story happen, things not so good for those mississauga. things not so good.

most people had enough food, so that wasn't it. not this time.

most people had houses, so that wasn't it. not this time.

most people were practicing their ways, that wasn't it. not this time.

this time it was with their neighbours. those ones that moved in beside them. they partying all the time. loud all the time. never taking care. tramping all over those plants mississauga use to heal. eating everything out of the mississauga's garden. building a big wooden deck fence all around the mississauga's house so nobody can get in and out no more. cutting down trees for no reason. peeing in the water.

that's right. they were peeing in the water.

i know.

can you imagine? what kinda people pee in the water?

but it was more than just pee. they could cut down all kinds of trees, put them into special machines and out comes birch bark. long, beautiful sheets of birch bark. but they don't make no canoes.

no siree. they put lines on it and then throw it away. that's what they did with most of the stuff they made. they throwed it away.

then they build a concrete river and a big elevator machine that lifts boats so they don't have to carry them over portages. i know. kinda magic eh? imagine. never having to portage around no more rough water.

well that big elevator machine, turns out it not so special after all. it not so magic. while all those white people just sailing down the concrete river riding up and down on that elevator machine, those shackles start to hurt the veins of mother earth. she starting to feel the pain. she starting to feel all locked up. can't move. things not flowing, getting everything all backed up. salmon and eels getting all traffic jammed up at those elevator machines, can't get to where they're going. everybody getting sick, even those animals and them fish, everybody. slow kinda sickness that one, sneaks up on you. those neighbours don't notice though, just keep riding that elevator machine. just keep making more.

hundred years go by, maybe more. the fish and the mississauga are sad and lonely and tough and mad and a lot of them, maybe even most of them, are dead. those neighbours have a big party to celebrate the elevator machine's birthday. cake. balloons. even invite those mississauga to sing, get kinda mad when no mississuaga show up, but anyway, party must go on.

and these mississauga, they tried everything. they had them neighbours over for dessert, try and be friends. rhubarb pie. that's what they all had. homemade. good stuff that biindigen wushk. the neighbours, they nice and they say,

"oh yes, yes yes. you are soooooo right. it will never happen again. you can trust us."

then, whoops, it happen again.

so those mississauga had those neighbours over for dinner, try and come up with some ground rules. the neighbours, they nice and they say,

"oh yes, yes yes. you are soooooo right. it will never happen again. you can trust us."

then, whoops, it happen again.

so the mississauga invite them over one more time for a serious discussion with no pie. just tea this time. this time those neighbours say,

"whoa whoa ... what you people getting your panties in a knot for? what you people doing being so uptight all the time? we just living our lives. doing our things. we can't stop riding our elevator machine or our economy fall apart and we have no health care and we get sick. you don't want us to get sick, do you, indians?"

mississauga don't want any ones to get sick. sick is no fun.

"everything is going to be ok, mississauga," those neighbours say.

"we do better. your river, she not so trampled. it's already coming back. see? you're making a big deal about nothing. we'll be more careful. it won't happen again." then those neighbours plant lawn and geraniums where mississauga medicine suppose to be.

whoops, it happen again.

mississauga starting to get mad. starting to think those neighbours not honourable. maybe doing a bit of lying. maybe trying to pull the wool over those mississauga eyes. so they have a big meeting and they don't invite the neighbours this time. binesiwag watching from above. everybody has ideas on what to do. but which idea going to work? that always the problem. somebody say,

"this idea going to work, this is the way to go, i'm sure of it."

then a woman say,

"what about this. you forgot about this. this is going to be a problem."

it goes around like that for a long time.

every time they get close to deciding, echo-maker fly over, booming and crashing, saying no, no, no. don't decide when you're all mad. don't decide too quick. take your time on this one. be smart. be strategic. sleep on it. go get massages first. then decide. everybody act nice after massages. clears the head and heart.

so those mississauga go and get massages. real nice kind with dim lights and new age wave music and flannel sheets.

in the meantime though, she, who is just a young one gets all frustrated with all the patience, massaging and talking. she, who is just a young one, decides to take things into her hands. she's heard those old ladies pray. she's seen them walk around those lakes. but this time, she puts her semaa down and she sings a different kind of prayer, and she don't say it to nibi, not this time. nope, she say it to binesiwag.

and those binesiwag heard that prayer and they had their own meeting. they know that elevator machine has got to go and they know who they got to talk with. except she is kinda snippy sometimes, that one. she do good work, but sometimes binesiwag maybe get a little jealous or offended or maybe that one that lives in the water maybe gets a little snippy and then next thing you know someone throws a rock or then maybe binesiwag calls her a monster and then maybe fight gets on.

so binesiwag gots to be careful. gots to go carefully down to that beach and give her name a call, all sweet like. maybe put out an offering. maybe sing that song she like, 'bout the time first striker didn't duck fast enough and lost a tail feather. maybe sing that one just to get her in a cushy mood.

but while binesiwag are deciding, taking their time, maybe going to get massages, echo-maker is flying around trying to get those mississauga to their massages before they make a bad decision, overseer goes down to the beach, puts an offering down and sings that song.

then she wait.

she wait and wait.

she wait and wait and wait.

she wait some more.

then she starting to get impatient. like maybe that one that lives in the water is there and just not coming up so she can see her. making her wait on purpose like.

overseer fly over to kaakaabiikaa to see what she can see. see if she see any signs of mishibizhiw.

the water get all choppy, and the wind gets all excited like maybe something going to happen, sky gets all grey coloured.

"hola what happened to my sunny day? binesiwag gimme my sunny day back! i'm working on my tan because i have a hot date tonight. got a new fancy party dress, going to that new place to eat, and i want my sunny day back."

"oh, why aaniin, mishibizhiw, so nice to see you. i know you gotta get all dolled up in that new party dress. i'll give you your sunny day back, don't you worry. you'll get your sunny day back in time for your tan and your date. but first i need you to do something for me."

overseer gets out some candy and gives it to mishibizhiw. everybody wants to be a helper after candy. overseer butters mishibizhiw up.

"this job really, really important. the survival of the lake and the river and everything depend upon it. the survival of the missis-sauga depend upon it. the survival of mishibizhiw and binesiwag depend upon it. and you, mishibizhiw, are the only one smart enough, fast enough and with enough sucking power to do it."

mishibizhiw eats up the candy.

"hey overseer, how about licorice next time. red, not the black."

"ok mishibizhiw, next time licorice."

mishibizhiw thinks about overseer's request.

"i am really fast. and i am very smart, and nobody, i mean noooobody can suck like me. it's true"

"yep it is. now pay attention. i need you to swim down the river until you get to liftlock 21. then stop."

"liftlock 21? the nationalism historical site of wonder?"

"ehn"

"the highest hydraulic liftlock in the world?"

"that's the sucker, sucker."

"easy."

"i hope you're not going to ask me to dig. i just got my nails done. like the colour?"

"oh yes. the colour is perfect, blueberry, na?"

"ehn its blueberries all right."

"i fix your nails if you have to dig, ok. my auntie does nails, i get you a special deal. no problem. she do feet too."

"ok?"

"ok. so you get to the lift lock, and you got to be quiet and discreet."

"ok, then what?"

"the you suck and suck and suck. suck it all out, 'til it's gone. suck all them locks out, all the way through the system, 'til you get to the big lake."

"ok."

"ok."

"overseer?"

"yep?"

"do i got time for a little fun on the way home after all that sucking?"

"like what?"

"like maybe knock down that jail the teaching rocks are locked in?"

"i dunno. that going to make the neighbours really mad. that's another one of their nationalism picnic parks."

"the neighbours already really mad because their boat elevator is all gone."

"ok. maybe hit it by mistake with your tail on the way back out. then call me, i set that appointment up with my auntie for your nails and feet. i'll get you a real bargain."

so now those mississauga just coming out of echo-maker's massage parlour, no not parlour, massage therapy clinic, when they see some kind of strange blue light off in the distance, at the base of the mountain sort of imploding, maybe getting sucked into the ground, like a big vacuum just under the surface. their eyes a little blurry from all that dim light and that padded toilet seat you put your face in at the massage place. they think they not seeing right.

but when they get home, them neighbours all gone. no house, no lawn, no geraniums, no fence even. like they were never there. like they got abducted by aliens or something, like they were never there. erased. gone. kaput. like maybe it all just a bad dream. mississauga sit down in their house all relaxed, have some tea, maybe a snack, try to remember what they were doing before those neighbours showed up.

---

nishnaabemowin: aanjibines means transformer or renewer, nahow is ok, biindigen wushk is rhubarb, kaakaabiikaa is a waterfall, mishibizhiw is a large, underwater lynx and binesiwag are thunderbirds.

she sang them home

bozhoo odenaabe
shki maajaamegos ndizhinaakaz
it's been a long time.

oowaah
odenaabe

oowaah
odenaabe

it's this way, i can feel
my lateral line drawing forward

let me let me let me
taste you

oowaah that feels good on my gills

my kobade told her daughter about that feeling
my great grandmother told her daughter
my kookum told her daughter
and my doodoom told me.

it was better than they said.

i've never felt like this
this is the perfect place
it's easy here

oowaah odenaabe odenaabe odenaabe odenaabe

bubbling
beating
birthing
breathing

bubbling
beating
birthing
breathing

oowaah odenaabe
i never thought we'd meet.

careful with me odenaabe
i'm not strong like those old ones.
they fasted and swam up here every year
this is my first time
weweni odenaabe
weweni

there are more coming from chi'nibiish
they're waiting at the mouth.

chi'nibiish
saagetay'achewan
pimadashkodeyaang
odenaabe
kitchi gaming
atigmeg zaageguneen
asin saagegun

asin saagegun
atigmeg zaageguneen
kitchi gaming
odenaabe
pimadashkodeyaang
saagetay'achewan
chi'nibiish

you're quicker than i thought

is jijaak still here?
i hope jijaak.
an old one told me about
"land of jijaak and migizi" she said.

don't worry odenaabe
your wounds from the shackle locks

from the dams
they'll heal now they're gone

we're bringing pimizi
we bringing all the ones that are gone

it's over now
you can cry now

it's over
we're all going to be ok now

they're gone.

and there is more of us waiting to be born.

nishnaabemowin: bozhoo odenaabe is hello otonabee, shki maajaamegos ndizhi-naakaz means my name is new trout that leaves (salmon), odenaabe is the otonabee river that boils and bubbles and beats like a heart, weweni means carefully, doodoom is a name for mother used by children, meaning "my breastfeeder," kobade is link, great grandmothers, great grandchildren, chi'nibiish is lake ontario, saagetay'achewan is trent river, pimadashkodeyaang is rice lake, gichi gaming is katchewanooka lake, asin saagegun is stoney lake, atigmeg zaageguneen is clear lake.

for asinykwe

*t*his story takes place a long time ago or maybe right now. the world was thrown. the mother was shaken so hard that everything cracked. shattered. we cracked. everything fell to the ground in thousands of pieces. and when everything hit the ground the pieces flew through the air scattered all over everywhere.

no one knew what to do.

some people didn't survive.
some people gave up. moved on. buried. forgot.
some people found ways to cope.
some people worked hard at just breathing. just breathe.

maybe it went on a few generations like this. just holding on.
waiting for something better.
just breathing.

then there was a woman. an ogichidaakwe, but not yet. she started traveling around our territory and in the west, picking up those things that we'd forgotten. picking up all those shattered pieces of nishnaabewin that had been taken from us, or lost or forgotten. she had a big black ash basket that she used to pick up these things. and so she traveled around visiting with the old people. and at first the old people in her own community were too busy to help her. but she persisted, and she was led out to the west. she found old people there that remembered their stories, the ceremonies, their dances. she recorded and memorized and learned those ways until she knew them in her heart, and into her basket they would go. then she came back to the east, and she started waking up those old people that had forgotten. what about this? who remembers about that? she recorded and memorized and learned those ways until she carried them in her heart, and into her basket they would go.

by the time she got here, to michi saagiig nishnaabeg territory, she had a big basket full of songs, stories, ceremonies, a language we'd almost forgotten. she came here because of all the gizhiikatig and those teaching rocks. she came here to work with our young women. she came here with seeds to plant, and she planted them in our soil. she took care of them. and over time, those seeds grew into the most beautiful flower garden you've ever seen—roses, makazin flowers, trilliums, pitcher plants.

her voice healed us every time we heard it.

those that could see quietly called her "the woman who changed our nation," because she woke us up, and she's got so much humility she doesn't even know it.

she never asked for any recognition, because she wasn't doing it to be recognized. she did it because it filled her up.

she just carefully planted those seeds.
she just kept picking up those pieces.
she just kept visiting those old ones.
she just kept speaking her language and sitting with her mother.

she just kept on lighting that seventh fire every time it went out.

she just kept making things a little bit better, until they were.

nishnaabemowin: nishnaabewin is the nishnaabe way of life, ogichidaakwe is a holy woman, gizhiikatig is cedar, michi saagiig nishnaabeg are mississauga nishnaabeg and our territory is the north shore of lake ontario, makazin flowers are lady slippers.

a love song for attawapiskat

they fed me one story
then another,
spinning it
until
it became
the unraveling ball of wool,
it always was.

white lies are like that.

but me
i see different
because
i have no home
to keep feelings like these.

on my tv,
i saw your kid's
big brown eyes
carry light
across the frame.

i saw the corner
of gwezens' shy smile
carry 10 000 years
of benevolence.

i saw those chubby
brown toddler legs,

and fat rosy cheeks
full of doodoo.

i saw the lines
on that kookum's face,
the ones that trace

you from
the beginning of time.
the one whose body
is a magnificent
instrument of story.

on my tv,
i heard that
auntie's silence.
because you can hear silence
if you try.

i heard your
elders
your dancers
your musicians
your poets.

i heard your
berry pickers
your beaders
your story-tellers
your kookums.

i heard your
hunters
your trappers
your fishers
your medicine people.

on my tv
i held the sound of your big river
crashing
rushing
birthing
life over land
birthing
life over diamond rings
birthing
life over sewage.

i held that brave one's
young voice
on the stolen hill
telling the gimaa that never listens
the gimaa that can't listen
the gimaa that refuses to listen
that she needs a school.

and in your bright blue sky
above the cold that cracks bone,
i carried with me
a lone canadian flag
missing its spine,
one red stripe
shredded and lost,
the other,
blowing away
in the breath
of the parting rocks.

gwekaanimad

*b*iindigen. namadabin. oowaah. good to see you. i'll get the tea. watch your feet. don't let that one nip you in the toes. gotta watch your feet with that one. he bark too much too. i'll get the tea. that'll start the story off good. gotta start that story off in the right direction because you don't want it getting away from you. you don't want it going somewhere you don't want it to go. get into all kinds of trouble, that one. gotta keep a hold of that story. start it off right. like the way it happened. don't want it to start thinking it is all kinds of a big deal, big shot, that one. tricky one, that story.

i got an auntie, you see. some things, she is right about. some things. when she's right she's right. some things, she's not so right about. maybe not so right about all the hiding. all the scared. maybe not right about putting on all those costumes, dressing up. being something she isn't, pretending all the time. telling her kids to pretend, so they could tell their kids. maybe not so right about that part. maybe not so right about wanting everything to be easy all the time either. drinking all that medicine so she floats all the time. floating, instead of walking. oowaah. maybe not so right about that part. but some things, she right about. and maybe some of those things important. big things. big important things. she say don't walk down those white people streets with your head held high. don't go flaunting yourself. you'll pay. they'll make you pay those ones. not a safe thing to do, not a good thing to do. don't go doing that she say. and she keep safe, so maybe she right about that one. she keep safe her whole life. eighty years she kept safe, that old auntie of mine. oowaah. she's an old lady that one.

nahow, but that's not this story that one. that's another story. different story. different kind of story, that one. this story is about a parade. big parade. big nishnaabeg parade. how about that? ever think you'd see that? big nishnaabeg parade? that auntie of mine, she say that'd never happen. them big shots never allow that to happen. only white people have parades. parades are for white people, that's what she say. white people like parades. they put up them metal fences so the watchers can't dance down the street too. they in the parade. we the watchers. they always gotta have watchers, white people. always looking over their shoulder, nearly missing the parade, nearly tripping. auntie says them watchers keep those white people heads big. that's how she says it, that one.

back to that parade. that big nishnaabeg parade. happened last month, ode'min giizis them old people call it. all about heart berries that one. and you know those berries they got them roots and runners. all entwined. hard to pick its roots that one. all connected underground. those berries, they a women's medicine. and there's this very important woman in this story. she important because she have a vision. a big vision. lotta people have big ideas though, big visions. maybe too many people got big ideas. but this one, she special. she a special women 'cause she not just have a big vision, she act.

she work hard that woman. talking. negotiating. convincing. she go everywhere that one and she talk to everyone. all those big shots. not all those big shots think her idea good. and sometimes she get mad that one, 'cause nobody listening. everybody too busy. everybody gotta go shopping. everybody busy with dragon boats and wake boards and working on their tans. she never give up though, because she knows we can do better. we all can do better. she tells us "do better." and we kind of scared of that woman, because she right. we can do better. then she makes this great big festival where we all gotta show we better. but it's not just about that. it's a party too. big party. big nishnaabeg party. big party celebrating big things. like we're still here. that kind of a big party. and she says that this time, at this party, we're not the watchers. that's an important thing she say. we're not the watchers. in fact, this party so big, there are no watchers. imagine that. a party with no watchers.

so this woman, nishnaabekwe let's call her. she says we going to make a big parade and we going to hold up our heads high and we going to walk down the main street of nogojiwanong. she tells the big shots. she tells the police. she says come if you want police and you know, some of them come. she get all them kids together and teaches them to make birds. all them kids make this big flock of birds, birds like you've never seen. with sparkles and rainbow feathers and glittery eyes and that paper that floats on the air. them kids make all these beautiful birds for the big parade. them bineshiinyag, they gonna fly in the parade and they going spread all kinds of seeds all around, and them seeds going to grow into something. you'll see. them seeds going to grow into some big pretty garden with tasty things too. remember that first time? them bineshiinyag, they spread them seeds real good and make gzhe manidoo gitigan. oowaah that was beautiful! remember that? oowaah.

then that nishnaabekwe, she gets an even bigger idea. and she act on that idea too, and the next thing you know there are bigger than life puppets, take two maybe three people to move those ones. she say they going to make everyone feel good. even those ones that refuse to come. even those ones that can't be anything but the watchers. they gonna see these big puppets and their hearts are going to fill up and then gonna feel happy whether they want to or not. they gonna get swept away. that's what she say, that nishnaabekwe.

so the big day come. everyone gather. the kids got all them birds. the people got those big puppets. maybe some of them on stilts so they really tall. some women, they bring their drums. some men, they bring that big drum, too. some people dress up real nice and dance. but we all there. we all come. that nishnaabekwe there too and she look real happy, that one. like the kind of happy no one can steal from you. that kind of big happy that those ones can't steal.

and that nishnaabekwe she say aambe! maajaada! and we all hear her, and maybe we a bit scared, but she say aambe! maajaada! and we go. and we put our heads up high just like she saw in her dream. and we dance down that street of ours. and we not the watchers. we the doers. and that turtle, she likes it that day. she likes all those gentle brown feet massaging her back. oh that feel good. little lower maybe. maybe to the right just a bit. no, no not that far. aaahh. that right. right there. that turtle like that massage. she like everyone singing her song.

and that tricky one, he come to the parade too. maybe he was teasing around a bit. making sure we not taking ourselves too seriously. maybe he help create that great big spectacle. maybe he help nishnaabekwe create that great big red spectacle. and maybe he help us parade down that street a bit. maybe pulling on someone's hair and then running away. maybe touching another's shoulder and then vanishing. maybe blowing a bit of smoke in someone's eyes, that one. oowaah. that one, he funny.

ma'iingan, she there too that day. she walk with the people. beside. side by side. brushing their legs or maybe touching shoulder to shoulder. maybe not moving, just touching. waiting to see who'd move away first, that one. but the people never did, not that day. no one moved. they just touched. touched and walked.

and those others ones came too. the ones with wings and the ones with hooves and the ones with paws. they came and they lined that street. that street all those nishnaabeg parade down. they wove themselves in the crowd. they stood there. i saw them with my own eyes. just standing there. just still. just present. they lined that whole street, those ones. aahh. they felt good those ones. no one forgot them that day. they looked us in the eye that day. you know when that one, maybe a special one, looks you in the eye, and maybe for just a second you don't look away. maybe for a second you just let yourself look back. and then maybe you feel something. something good. something that maybe you think you aren't suppose to feel, maybe something you didn't feel for a long time. and for that second you get all filled up with that special one. that one that makes you stay when you should go. full of potential. full of hope. full of love. and you fill yourself up with as much of that special as you can. and then you just keep walking. you just hold your head up high and you keep walking.

walking instead of floating.

---

nishnaabemowin: gwekaanimad means shifting wind, biindigen means come in, namadabin means sit down, nahow is ok, bineshiinyag are birds, gzhwe manidoo gitigan is the creator's garden, ma'iingan is a wolf, ode'min giizis is strawberry moon or the month of june, nishnaabekwe means ojibway woman, and aambe! maajaada! is come on! let's go!

acknowledgements

the beginning quote from lee maracle is from the poem "blind justice" published in *decolonization: indigeneity, education & society.*

"decolonial love" is taken from an interview with junot díaz in the *boston globe* called "the search for decolonial love."

the first four subtitles in "smallpox, anyone" are names of work by rebecca belmore. the last line of the poem is from her performance "i quit."

the title "lost in a world where he was always the only one" was suggested by john k. samson.

the title "it takes an ocean not to break" is a line from the song "terrible love" by the national.

the line "only drunks and children tell the truth" in the story "buffalo on" is the title of a play by drew hayden taylor.

the story "gezhizhwazh" was influenced by cbc ideas broadcast and transcript of an interview with caroline anderson and roger roulette in 2003.

chi'miigwech to bonnie devine for the cover art. miigwech to ursula pflug, tara williamson and steve daniels for encouragement, insightful comments and careful editing on previous drafts. many thanks to john k. samson who put a considerable amount of thought and kind energy into the stories throughout the writing process. miigwech to ryan mcmahon for reminding me to go towards fear, not away from it. miigwech to dory nason, taiaiake alfred, ansley simpson and shannon simpson for letting me run things past them at the very last minute. thanks as well to lee maracle and waubgeshig rice. chi'miigwech to doug williams for help on nishnaabemowin, and the names of lakes and rivers in "nogojiwanong." thanks also to rick wood, sarah michaelson and the folks at arp books.

thanks to the leighton artist colony at the banff centre, the canada council for the arts, the ontario arts council's writers' reserve for their support.

thanks to several editors for publishing earlier versions of some of these stories. "gwekaanimad" was published in *the link*, an early version of "birds in a cage" under the title "heavy metal girls" was published in the *ode'min giizis literary supplement*. "she told him 10 000 years of everything" was published as "sabe" in *briarpatch magazine*, as the winner of their writing from the margins short fiction contest. "nogojiwanong: she hid him in her bones" was published under the title "ice fishing" in *kimiwan zine*. "identity impaired" and "smallpox, anyone?" were also published by *kimiwan zine*. "lost in the world where she was always the only one" was published by *muskrat magazine*. "smallpox, anyone?," "pipty" and "ishpadinaa" were all published by *rice paper literary magazine*. "leaks" was published in *decolonization: indigeneity, education & society*. "jiibay or aandisoke" was published in *that not forgotten*, edited by bruce kauffman and published by hidden press books. "nogoji-wanong: she is the only doorway into this world" under the title "untitled" was installed as part of *jiigbiing* at the art gallery of pe-terborough. "nogojiwanong: she sang them home" was included under the title "maajaamegos ndizhinakaaz" as an audio piece as part of *jiigbiing*. "maajaamegos ndizhinakaaz" was also choreo-graphed into a dance piece by rulan tangen and performed in zhishodewe … at the water's edge. a different version of "nogoji-wanong: she asked them for help" was published in the *gift is in the making* (highwater press, 2013), under the title "good neighbours." "treaties" was published by *geist*. "spacing" was published in *as us literary journal*.

islands of decolonial love
leanne betasamosake simpson
& friends

download or stream music/spoken word album at
arpbooks.org/islands

she hid him in her bones
(music written and preformed by nick ferrio)

leaks
(music written and preformed by tara williamson)

smallpox, anyone
(music written and preformed by sarah decarlo)

identity impaired
(music written and preformed by melody mckiver)

jiibay or aandizooke
(instrumental "woodcarver" by a tribe called red)

spacing
(music written and performed by sean conway)

ishpadinaa
(traditional women's song performed by leanne betasamosake
simpson)

she sang them home
(instrumental "war cry movement I" by cris derksen)

a love song for attiwapiskat
(instrumental "war cry movement II" by cris derksen)

nick ferrio, *dobro*
tara williamson, *piano and vocals*
sarah decarlo, *keyboard*
melody mckiver, *viola*
a tribe called red *instrumental from "woodcarver"*
sean conway, *guitar*
leanne betasamosake simpson, *vocals*
cris derksen, *war cry movement I*
cris derksen, *war cry movement II*

instrumentals and poetry for all tracks except spacing and the works by a tribe called red and cris derksen were recorded at the narrows with sound engineer james mckenty. spacing was recorded by chris culgin at ephram. all tracks were mixed by james mckenty and mastered by harris newman at greymarket mastering.

special thanks to: steve daniels, tara williamson, nick ferrio, james mckenty, john k. samson, chris culgin, cara mumford, rulan tangen, minowe simpson, nishna simpson, marrie mumford, sarah decarlo, melody mckiver, sean conway, ryan mcmahon, jarrett martineau, eric ritskes, sara roque, cris derksen, a tribe called red, doug williams, patti shaughnessy, susan blight, indigenous waves radio, aaron mason, aaron mason photography and the aboriginal arts program of the ontario arts council.

leanne betasamosake simpson

leanne betasamosake simpson is a writer and academic of mississauga nishnaabeg ancestry. she is the editor of *lightning the eighth fire: the liberation, protection and resurgence of indigenous nations* (arp books) and *this is an honour song: twenty years since the blockades* (with kiera ladner, arp books). she is the author of *dancing on our turtle's back: stories of nishnaabeg re-creation, resurgence and a new emergence* (arp books) and *the gift is in the making: anishinaabeg stories* (debwe series, highwater press). she lives in mississauga nishnaabeg territory.